T0121524

asleep

awake

asleep

asleep

awake

asleep

stories

Jo-Ann Bekker

Published in 2019 by Modjaji Books
Cape Town, South Africa
www.modjajibooks.co.za

Edited by Alison Lowry
Cover text and artwork by Jesse Breytenbach
Book layout by Andy Thesen
Set in Berling

ISBN print: 978-1-928215-78-3
ISBN ebook: 978-1-928215-79-0

To Guy, Leo, David

Contents

1

2

3

4

5

6

Although its math is precise, time has the texture of magic.
– Lily Hoang

All fiction is the factual refracted.
– Ivan Vladislaviç

1

Dolphins left a chocolate in the fridge

The dolphins left a chocolate in the fridge. I tear open the stapled wrapper and finish it in two bites. Crumbly, with chewy bits.

My younger son tells me what to eat.

Last year he was a first-team rower and lived on chicken and mince. He told me to eat more protein and I devoured the flesh of baby sheep. I sucked the marrow from their bones.

This year my son is a dolphin. He meditates. He lives on grains and plants. He brought the dolphins to stay for the varsity holidays and we made lacto-fermented sauerkraut. I bought cacao, goji berries and chia seeds to make raw chocolates. I cooked vegetable curries. I missed chicken.

I know how this makes me sound. I know about the gap between rich and poor in my town. I see the starving people staggering from the soup kitchen. The unemployed men queuing for piecemeal work. The homeless people who sleep in the church grounds before spiky fences lock them out. I know why the car guard at the post office gives me the middle finger.

I know most superfoods are imported. I know about food-miles. About methane emissions.

I know the lagoon is in the distance, but it looks so close, so clear.

Every leaf on every tree sparkles.

The sky is loudly blue.

The dining table stretches away from me. My lips buzz. My

feet tingle. I feel nauseous. The cat jumps onto the table and puffs out his fur. I can see every black and grey striped hair on his body. Each one ends in a white tip. I can see the space between each fibre-optic hair. The fur parts to reveal a white opening – not a wound, not a scar, more an entrance.

I think of touching it but lie down instead.

I pick up my phone but my sons are offline.

My younger son and I are on good terms. We are closer than when he was twelve and wrote *Mom Mom she screams a lot but she's the only food source I've got* on my Mother's Day card. Than when he was fourteen and came home with his friends in the back of a police van, reeking of booze. Than when he was fifteen and told us he wanted to go to boarding school: *I would rather feel scared every day than stay at home and feel nothing.* When he told his new principal: *I need to get away from these people*, meaning Jay and me.

I am a mother who swoops and frets. He is a son who tells us nothing. Until he goes to university and tells us everything.

He talks about the trance festivals the dolphins attend. How they dance all day and all night. How they help him feel so much love for everyone and everything. How he climbed a hill alone and took off his clothes and understood that we are all one with everything. Everything is one. His words turn into images. I can see him sitting naked in the sun, feel how the bushes scraping his skin seem gentle. I listen and smile while my maternal soundtrack plays anxious violins.

Jay loves these conversations. Jay is obsessed with the paranormal and near-death experiences. He is fascinated by trance ceremonies and is considering an ayahuasca retreat. I find this odd because Jay has never been that interested in mind-altering substances. Marijuana leaves him speechless. He prefers alcohol, measured out carefully each night into beer, wine or whisky glasses.

Lying on the couch I start laughing. Jay should have eaten the chocolate.

3

The two wingback chairs near the couch have hazy outlines. They are hovering, shimmering auras. Haloes. Everything in the open-plan lounge and kitchen is recognisable but heightened. Skewed. The ceiling looks wavy, pleated.

The clouds outside are massing. The door onto the deck has four glass panels. I watch cumulus clouds through one panel. I see faces in the billowing clouds. Plump faces with bulging cheeks. My top lip wants to lift. I lift it, curl it up. I move my mouth, open it wide, and the cloud people move their mouths as well. I stretch my mouth and they stretch theirs.

There is a transparent veil behind the wingback chairs. A luminous shimmering film flecked with hundreds of small rainbows. The colours grow stronger. The veil becomes electric green. I see everything through kaleidoscopes, compound vision. Everything is repeated. Everything has defined honeycomb edges.

I close my eyes.

A vibrant sun-drenched landscape of small, soft sea anemones. Each round segmented organism is composed of different colours and differently shaped parts. Each creature is moving and changing. An endless expanse of soft coral or inter-tidal succulents evolving into different creatures and different vistas.

On the outside deck Jay's dream catcher and a string of solar lights hang from the roof. The globes rock slowly in the wind. The sky is blue. The tips of the candlewood trees sway to and fro.

A landscape of low curved dwellings. Day-glo colours. Flashes of ultraviolet light.

A vista of round shapes with pink neon outlines.

Continents of intricate cubes and rectangular prisms in different sizes, with yellow, green or orange fluorescent surfaces.

A world of metal components more elaborate than any motherboard.

A realm of thin curving paper-clips, just a few highlighted with scribbles of metallic colour.

A pinprick of light, just off centre.

The solar lights and dream catcher are suspended from the deck of an American beach house. Then they are hanging from a thatched shelter on a tropical island. The sky darkens with the looming storm, shimmers with rain, burns with the sunset. The candlewood tree tops are evenly spaced sentinels, they are marching soldiers.

I laugh. I understand everything. The fascination with kaleidoscopes. The attraction to ultraviolet lights, day-glo colours, mirror balls. I understand all art: gargoyles, cubism, pop art, Van Gogh's multi-coloured brush strokes.

A grey space. A place like an underground parking garage. Another place like the cold functional space before an underground lift. Ugly unlit spaces. Places where violence happens. Breathe in, breathe out.

Pink sky, the dream catcher with its fake crystal, the rocking string of solar lights, the swaying tree tops.

A blue-black world. Everything is swirling. No light. People. A vertical line of elongated people, one on top of the other. Interacting. I think of Jay telling me about near-death experiences which describe a ladder to the next world. I want to tell him it is not a ladder. There are no rungs, no levels, no platforms. It is more like a chain. A chain of people like in Blake's paintings.

I am watching the vertical people when I realise I might have eaten a wild mushroom. It might be poisonous. I might be dying. I can see my mother hovering nearby, my frail mother who is ready to die. I don't speak to her and she doesn't see me. I need to focus. Prepare for dying. I inhale slowly, exhale. I feel okay. My family will be fine. I have completed what I have completed. Then I remember I ate a chocolate, the dolphins' chocolate.

I open my eyes. The lounge is crimson, golden, bright. Heaven. An illusion. No more substantial than the grey place or the dark blue place.

A stranger hovers near the fireplace, a stooped man. There is someone behind him.

A frieze of people, all standing side by side, holding hands, a string of paper dolls cut from a folded sheet of paper.

A few stick-like creatures with sparse hair. Groups of very short beings.

A bottlenose dolphin, a kind caring presence.

Faces in a circle or wheel. Faces I recognise. The shoeless man who walks beside the lagoon arguing with the air. The car guard from the post office. The young woman who cleans our house twice a week. My university lecturer. They all look happy. I see my son standing to one side watching me. I lift my upper lip. I can feel my son by changing the shape of my mouth. I become him, I move my mouth and become the people on the wheel. The wheel is spinning, all the faces are spinning. We are all dissolving into one.

I live through my curling lip, through my mouth. The cool air on my teeth and gums feels good. I see something to the left of the wheel. Something scruffy with fur and teeth. I lift my upper lip, stretch my lower jaw down. I am opening my mouth like a rat. If I turn and look at the animal I will realise it is me. I choose not to look.

The light above the dishwasher has been switched on. I see Jay in the kitchen. I call him, my voice slow but steady, normal.

'I'm fine. If you're hungry there is butternut soup in the fridge.'

Each sound is magnified. The neighbour's dog barking outside, the hotplate on the stove clicking as it heats up the soup. The firewood crackles, pops, sizzles.

I keep thinking it is over but then I start tingling again, my upper lip buzzes. Sensations build up: gradual, gentle, lovely. I snuggle down into the couch. The sleeping bag stretches away from me like a blue pupa. My phone vibrates, I am surprised to see it in my hand. I stare at the glowing screen. It looks alive.

The usually scratchy wool cushion beneath my cheek feels warm, soft, subtly textured. The fake fur trim on my coat's hood is a silky animal.

I am a spongy sea creature with millions of tentacles of feeling, expanding, pulsing. Breathing deeply enhances the tingling. Pleasure spreads everywhere and is concentrated in an arbitrary point of contact: where my hip bone touches the couch. The slightest adjustment causes seismic shifts of sensation.

A whoosh of warm healing rushes through me like liquid, like light. Blasts through my stomach, through my right breast and out, cleansing me, healing me, clearing any blockages. I feel scoured, deliciously empty, completely alive. I need nothing. No food. No water.

There is still tingling but the vistas are less populated, the colours restricted to just a glimpse here and there.

I open my eyes and the sky outside is black. The wingback chairs look dull, diminished. I have pins and needles in my fingers. Jay is drinking whisky beside the fire.

❖

An olive thrush takes a sunlit gap through trees, flies fast, head first, into the deck's glass door. Crashes to the tiled floor. Crouches on its belly with cocked head. Eyes glazed, unblinking. One wing unfurled. Motionless.

All the birds I have rescued from cats and windows, placed in boxes, fed sugar water. The birds I buried. The few who recovered, who flew around the room losing feathers, bashing at every pane until they found an open window.

I leave the thrush alone.

The cat is asleep on the couch, I am at the table. I can see the brain-damaged thrush if I look up from my book. The words on the page are still. Last night they glowed, as if backlit. As if just a few words were enlarged in bold, leaping out of the sentences.

The words keep still but phrases whisper. *The Sick Rose; each charter'd street; the charter'd Thames, these Satanic Mills.* Blake's London sounds like my town.

I check the time, my younger son is still in lectures.

I turn to the illustrations, to Jacob's Ladder. It is a staircase, not a chain of people. But they are my people. The elongated people I saw.

I turn to an image of an empty hall and at the end of the hall an empty cubicle with a desk where a poet is writing, taking dictation from an angel.

My desk looks onto trees and water and hills. A garden wild with long grasses and overgrown bitou and taaibos. An unkempt garden with flowering thistles and plants many called weeds. The garden Jay made for birds. The birds who fly into our windows. There are sunbirds in the wild dagga, turaco eating essenhout berries. There is no wind, the candlewoods are still.

Blake's words: *Everything that lives is holy.*

I have killed fleas, ants, mosquitoes. Smashed two birds with my car, driven over one cat. I live easily alongside snakes, spiders and scorpions but have an aversion to rats. I was born in the year of the rat. I will roast chicken for supper. I will eat the anus while I carve, sit down to consume the thighs.

The thrush lifts its head, tucks in its wing. It hops forward, then waits. Then it is on the railing, spreading its wings, swooping over the hedge.

I pick up my phone to text my son. I put it down.

2

Transplanted

Just before she sailed home on a mail ship, a woman met a younger man.

There was something about him. His bare feet at parties. His laugh. The way he kissed. She sailed home to buy a wedding dress and sailed right back.

The woman was happy with her husband but unsettled in his land. The unsettled land where shots rang out. Where those with uniforms and guns stood, where those with tattered clothes and bullets lay. The woman and her husband scooped up their firstborn and boarded the mail ship. They sailed north for weeks until they reached the wife's cold land. The husband tried to stay but yellow fog engulfed the streets. He couldn't breathe. They scooped up their daughter and her tiny sister and sailed back to the sun.

They lived in a city with beaches and mountains. The husband sold treats. He drove his company car and stopped at shops with separate doors and separate counters for separated people. The husband walked through the front doors. He unwrapped chocolate bars of nougat and caramel and chocolate slabs with creamy mint bubbles and offered the shopkeepers a taste. The shopkeepers ordered cartons of slabs and bars – and they ordered packets of toffees and boiled sweets to sell from their shops' back doors.

The wife waited for her husband to come home. She cooked and cleaned and baked and sewed and planted flowers. She kissed and fed and washed and read and sang to her daughters. She watched them play in the sand, held their hands in shallow waves.

The husband sold so many treats he was promoted. He had to travel to isolated towns near farms and railway sidings. He rented an old house on a grape farm for his family. He told his wife he would be home on weekends.

The wife was sad to leave the sea, but she packed their belongings. She knitted jerseys for the inland cold. The husband found a playschool for their firstborn. He helped unpack their boxes and hang their curtains. Then he drove away in his company car filled with samples of treats.

The salesman's wife kept to herself on the farm. She kept apart from the farmer and his family, she stayed away from their big house. She didn't speak their language, the language of her daughter's nursery school. She refused to learn the language. She told the farmer she would do her own housework but he said he would send her a girl.

The girl was a woman called Jane. A slim woman who arrived at the kitchen door. The farmer's wife was with her. The farmer's wife opened the sink cupboard and took out a tin cup and bowl. The farmer's wife said these are for the girl. She likes black tea with sugar and thick bread with jam. The salesman's wife looked at Jane. Jane looked down. Jane ate her lunch on the kitchen doorstep.

Jane cleaned the house while the salesman's wife sewed cotton dresses. Jane fetched milk from the dairy and the wife scooped off the top layer and made ice-cream. Jane carried heavy baskets of grapes into the kitchen for the salesman's family.

The salesman and his wife played tennis on neighbouring farms on Saturday afternoons. But his wife would not join the wives' tea parties or gardening clubs or knitting circles. She said she was busy with her children. She ignored advice to just leave the kids with the girl.

The salesman's wife told her daughters stories about her homeland. How she caught snowflakes on her mittens, served her dolls sweets shaped like miniature fruit and vegetables, walked to school for morning and afternoon classes. She unpacked her wedding dress of broderie anglaise, let her children try on her veil and high-heeled shoes.

The wife savoured isolation but her daughters enjoyed company. The farmer's wife had a young son. The salesman's wife agreed to bring her girls for morning tea. She stayed for just one cup, accepted just one soetkoekie, but when she took her girls back home the boy came too.

The wife made chicken mayonnaise sandwiches for her daughters and the farmer's son. She placed Jane's jam sandwiches in the tin bowl and left it on the kitchen counter. She gave the children orange squash. She poured boiling water over the tea-bag in Jane's tin cup. She watched her daughter talking to the boy in a language she couldn't understand. She watched them play in the sun, they asked for water and she filled a bucket with the garden hose. Then she carried her toddler inside for a nap. The wife made her own lunch – a sandwich, tea, two blocks of chocolate – and ate while reading her library book in the sun. She closed her eyes for just a moment.

When she woke, the children were gone. Jane was walking towards her. Jane was holding out her tin bowl, a bowl filled with water and soggy bread.

The wife ran to the new farmhouse. She followed children's voices along a passage to a room with a closed door. She twisted the handle, grabbed her daughter's arm and dragged her into the passage. She pulled up her daughter's dress, pulled down her panties and planted her palm hard against the little bum – again and again and again.

Starlings

There are birds in the dairy's attic, you can hear them as you climb up the ladder after your friend. Your friend laughs like a waterfall. You want to be her, with a farm and horses and a house with a long stoep and a dairy with an attic. There are nests in the attic's straw. Nests with tiny chicks. Bald chicks calling for food with closed eyes and gaping beaks. And you know you shouldn't touch them, they're too young, but your friend takes a chick in each hand, crawls to the attic window and throws them down to the yard below. Throws them hard and they make red marks on the concrete. And you can't do it too. You don't protest, you just ask why. And she says birds bring lice and rats into the dairy and chucks another one out through the window.

Shards

He's home, I shout. I jump up. The spaniel at my feet panics, I trip over the dog and into the sunroom's door.

Benjy, the spaniel, has silky ears and poor eyesight. Time after time I walk through the front gate and he barks at me in an ugly way. I call out Benjy, Benjy, but he carries on barking until I reach the house. Then he suddenly recognises me and leaps into my arms. He licks my face and wags his stumpy tail.

My own dog is called Pom-Pom. She arrives with that name. She jumps out of the car and runs into our garden like it is her idea to come and live with us, nothing to do with the man who is selling her. I am disappointed at first because I wanted a puppy, then Pom-Pom smiles at me. I take her for walks and all the neighbourhood dogs come up and she smiles at them and they smile back. I build a jump course out of bamboo and she follows me around, jumping over every obstacle like a pony.

My sister's dog is Lily. Our cousins' Staffie has all these puppies and we get the runt of the litter. The puppy they call Lily the Pink. She is pretty but she snaps and snarls. When we go for walks Pom-Pom plays with other dogs and Lily gets jealous. She bares her teeth. Lily starts fights then changes her mind and withdraws, yelping, her tail between her legs.

On rubbish day all the dogs in the street bark madly. Lily rushes at the rubbish collectors, snapping at their heels. The men fling the heavy bags into the back of the rubbish truck and run after it. They have to run fast because the driver does not stop, he speeds up as the men are trying to jump back on. The men on the back of the truck shout and whistle encouragement and stretch their arms towards the running men. The dogs go wild. Lily comes home panting. A man in old clothes knocks on our door and shows us his bleeding leg. He tells our mother Lily bit him.

When we go on holiday our dogs go to the kennels. They each have their own cage. One year, Lily and Pom-Pom share a cage and Lily kills Pom-Pom. And the vet puts Lily to sleep.

My sister and I fight. We fight with words, hands and feet. We jab each other with our elbows in the car. Pinch each other hard under the table. We try to keep our faces blank, so our mother won't notice. Our worst fights are when we are alone. My sister always starts them. She is either spying on me, or laughing at me, or teasing me, or beating me at tennis. I sneer at her, or call her names, and she attacks me and I retaliate, and we carry on until we draw blood or cry or our mother shouts stop it stop it stop it.

On Sunday afternoons our parents go for a drive. Our baby brother goes with them. My sister and I stay at home and do homework and music theory. I am better at theory than piano. I am conscientious, but I don't have the touch. My sister has it, but she hates scales and theory. Once, as I'm correcting my theory, my sister grabs my rubber and won't give it back. I swat her with my textbook. The sharp corner hits her near her eye and leaves a mark. We say we hate each other. She says she is going for a bike ride. After I finish my homework, the doorbell rings. A strange woman is holding a mangled bike. My sister is standing beside her. She looks small and scraped. Her mouth is red. She gets a special filling for her chipped front tooth.

On holidays it is just us. We never go away with other families. One winter we hire a cabin in the mountains. While our parents unpack, we walk around the foothills. We walk until the grass is higher than our heads. The sun sinks behind the peaks. We stop fighting. We walk quietly. My sister walks behind me. Without speaking we know we are lost. We hold hands and cry. Then the long grass ends and we are back on the road. We run back to the cabin.

In December we go to the seaside. We run into the sea with our inflatable lilos. One minute we are riding the white water to the shore, the next my sister is being sucked out to sea. She looks scared. She is moving fast. I swim towards her and she stretches out her arm to me. Waves crash over us. A surfer pulls us onto his board and paddles us ashore.

We always hope to make friends on holiday. We walk up and down the beach looking for someone to play with. Usually we end up walking to the shop. If we take our brother with us, our mother gives us money for ice-creams. We push his pram and let it go and watch it move on its own, then we charge after it. It makes him laugh. One time we push the pram down the steep path outside the shop but it goes too fast, we can't catch up, it leaves the path and topples over onto the grass. Our brother sits up and laughs and so do we.

Last Christmas we got bikinis. A blue one for me, a brown one for my sister. My sister isn't even a teenager but she looks better in hers. We don't buy many ice-creams. We hardly look after our brother. We don't look for friends, they look for us. A swimmer chooses my sister. A swimmer whose father times him every morning as he does laps in the rock pool. My boy is tall and goofy. He does a backwards somersault off the veranda of our holiday bungalow. I know he is trying to decide between me and another, taller girl. But it is me he kisses on the beach. On the way back to the bungalows he talks to another boy about fish. He says: I think I hooked the right one. I go off him right away. The swimmer kisses my sister the following night. We are all sitting on the dune. The tall, goofy boy is talking to the taller girl. My sister loses her tooth filling.

I am too old to shriek and jump up but our father has been away for a fortnight. We are all excited. Our mother is in a good mood. The tea tray is set, the cake is waiting. There is

16

ice in the ice bucket, sherry and whisky on the drinks tray. My sister and brother are watching television but I am facing the sunroom's wall of glass. Autumn sun streams inside and the spaniel snoozes at my feet. I shout and leap up as the car glides down the driveway. Benjy wakes with a start. He barks and jumps up at me as I step towards the door. I fall over him and my right knee hits the door pane. The glass shatters: a jagged hole in the door, large shards of glass on the carpet and steps, smaller bits above and below my knee. My mother removes the pieces she can see, presses a wet cloth against the blood and we hobble to meet my father. He gets out of his car then gets back in and drives us to the hospital.

There is no pain until the doctor arrives, until he digs around in my wounds with tweezers and stitches up the cuts. The most painful part is the injection. The doctor says: Think of something nice. I go to the beach, to the closed eyes of the tall boy, to the clouds streaked and dotted across the dark sky, the moon racing between them.

Chosen

Belinda was different after Mr Marais kissed me in the art room. Before she looked happy when she sprinted off to hockey matches. Now her face seemed blotched.

Gemma changed too. Her arms twisted while she stood outside the music room.

Vanessa's eyes spoke as she passed by in the corridor, hugging her violin case.

The whispering in the classrooms increased. The sniggering.

No one had any proof. None of the gossiping girls. None of the parents who went to see the headmaster. The headmaster grinned and assured parents Mr Marais was a remarkable teacher who had done wonders for the choir and chamber orchestra.

There were twelve favourites, Mr Marais gave everyone a number. Belinda was number one. I was number two. He encouraged his chosen to stick together, to support one another, to show loyalty to him by working hard at school and being obedient daughters at home – even when parents criticised him.

Mr Marais's favourites spoke his first name like a mantra, discussed his shoulders, his chin, his voice, the instruments he played. He knew everything about music.

He knew little about art. It was a surprise to see him in the empty art room, to hear him say come into the storeroom. The bristles around his lips. The stink of his sweat. The speed at which he ran away afterwards.

Hypocrites

The smell of cassocks. Not the red cassocks Ripple and the other acolytes wore, the black cassocks of the priests. They smelt like her father's suits. When he was away Rip opened his cupboard and inhaled his jackets: pipe tobacco, Mum for Men, and something else. The cassocks smelt of cigarettes, strong deodorant and something else.

The smell of incense. Some girls said it made them want to faint, or hurl. Rip absorbed the cloying sweetness, grew heady, gazed up at the stained-glass light. *God from God, Light from Light ...*

The words. Their rhythm. The silences between phrases. The words she recited with the congregation *we have sinned against You, through our own fault ...* The dean's voice *pardon your sins and set you free from them, confirm and strengthen you in all goodness ...* The slow, hushed hymns *Just as I am ... O Lamb of God, I come.*

For a few seconds the words and light and incense filled her, stilled her. Then she'd be off again, thinking about the chocolate éclairs her parents would buy on the way home, scanning the pews in the congregation below for boys, gazing at Arthur in the opposite choir stall. *Almighty God unto whom all hearts are open, all desires known and from whom no secrets are hid ...*

Rip took her confirmation classes seriously. She learnt the Creed, contemplated the Trinity, tried not to covet.

The confirmation service was at night. The girls wore white, like brides. Rip had white shoes and stockings and a long-sleeved dress her mother made. The others wore beige shoes, new summer dresses, fluffy cardigans and tiny silver crosses around their necks. Rip had inherited a chunky gold cross, with a kink where her aunt had bitten it. Her aunt smoked and drank and swore and never went to church, but her mother said the cross was precious: eighteen carat gold. Its long gold chain kept looping itself over one of Rip's small breasts.

It was difficult to think about receiving the Holy Spirit when you were wearing the wrong things. It was difficult not to smile about the spitty way the bishop spoke. The girls sat directly beneath the pulpit and someone mentioned umbrellas. Rip bit her lips shaking with laughter.

Rip expected transcendence when the bishop laid his hands on her head. Or when he painted a cross on her forehead with oil, the secret sign she had joined the church. Or when she took her first communion: *this is my body which is given for you ... my blood which is shed for you ...* The wafer dissolved quickly, the wine tasted like her mother's Old Brown Sherry. *Just as I am, though tossed about/ With many a conflict, many a doubt ...*

Rip became one of the first girls to serve at the cathedral's altar. On Sundays all the acolytes would line up in their red cassocks and white cottas, holding their heavy candlesticks in the prescribed way, and follow the crucifer into the church. The deacons, priests and dean followed in their cassocks, surplices, stoles and chasubles. For Christmas and Easter services the dean's vestments were stitched with gold.

It was just an ordinary Sunday service when the heavy entrance door slammed shut. Rip hadn't heard a word of the sermon. Arthur had asked her on a date. She was wondering what to wear. She was trying not to smile as she sang *Love with every passion blending*. She was thinking about a beauty tip in *Diana* magazine: use raw egg white for shiny hair.

Rip jumped at the crash of the wooden door. There was a pause and then the doors of the entrance porch with their diamond shaped panes swung open. A man with messy hair and creased clothes stumbled in, holding on to the back pews.

The dean announced the next hymn and sang the first lines of *Guide me, O They Great Redeemer* extra loud. The man found an empty pew and sat hunched forward during all three verses. As the organ's warble faded the man lifted his head and shouted: 'Hypocrites.'

The word was slurred but clear. It hung in the silence. The man gripped the pew in front of him, pulled himself up and began swaying up the aisle.

'Hypocrites,' he spat. 'You're all bloody hypocrites.'

He was speaking to Rip. He was a prophet, speaking the truth. She was a fraud. She did not deserve to carry a candle or serve at the altar. Her face burned.

As the dean began the consecration *Lift up your hearts …* two ushers moved swiftly to escort the man down the aisle and out of the church. The man fought them and they had to drag him out, ranting. A third usher closed the door quietly behind them.

Rip took communion … *not worthy so much as to gather up the crumbs under your table.*

Before delivering the peace, the dean congratulated the congregation on ignoring the unfortunate interruption. He announced the final hymn and Arthur led the way down the aisle, holding the cross straight and high. Rip and the other acolytes followed behind, blowing out their candles as they emerged outside. The dean was at the back of the procession as usual. Rip's mother said he gave his wife an especially loving smile.

A few years later Rip went to university and took a course in comparative religion. By the end of the semester she was an atheist. She bought a black coat from a charity shop, had it dry-cleaned, and took it back to her residence room. Ripping off the plastic covering, the smell hit her. The smell of suits and cassocks. The smell of something else.

Lesson

A British oboe player came to the City of Roses. It wasn't what he expected. There were no wild animals. People either spoke in harsh accents he found difficult to understand or whispered in a language of complex sounds.

He didn't pass a single rose bush on his daily walk from the university to the performing arts complex in town. It took an hour. For most of the way he seemed to be the only pedestrian. Cars with one or two occupants sped past followed by old buses filled to capacity.

It was always a relief to arrive at the rehearsal room and take his seat beside an elderly oboist, between the flautists and clarinetists. The conductor would give him a nod to play an A so the other instruments could check their tuning.

The orchestra appreciated his presence. The concert master shuffled the schedule to include a series of oboe concertos. The programme flagged his achievements with the Leeds College Orchestra and Gilbert & Sullivan societies. Audiences leaned forward to listen and clapped and cried bravo. He bowed and played and played and bowed. Grey-haired matrons described his technique as flawless and his musicality as imaginative and touching.

A newspaper reporter from the English-language newspaper came to see him. She was young and soft. She asked him questions and wrote down everything he said in her notebook. She looked into his eyes.

'I don't know much about the oboe,' she said.

He said it was a double-reed wind instrument with a compass of two and a half octaves from B flat below middle C. But when he could see she didn't understand he spoke about double reeds instead. He told her they were attached to the mouthpiece and determined the quality of an oboe's sound. Serious oboists made their own reeds. There were French, English, German and Dutch methods of fashioning the cane. He swore by the American way which he learnt from Walter Jouvel who had recently returned to Israel's Philharmonic Orchestra.

The oboe player imported his cane from France. It took him a fortnight to get a new reed working properly. On average – when he circulated three to four double reeds – it would last only four weeks. His oboe, a French model, was six years old.

The reporter asked about his family and he said his father had listened to classical music and taken him to concerts. At school he sang in the choir and played the guitar and trumpet. Somewhere in his mid-teens he took up the oboe. He studied law for a short while, hated it, and made music his career.

He was a serious man – tall and thin with glasses, a moustache and curly hair cut short – but he made a joke and she laughed. He looked at her and she smiled. He talked until she stopped asking questions and then she left.

After his rehearsal ended he walked to the newspaper's building in the centre of town. He hesitated outside, polished his spectacles, checked his short-sleeved shirt was tucked in and went up to the reception desk. He gave the reporter's name and she came downstairs.

'Is there a problem?' she asked. 'I'm on deadline.'

The oboe player cleared his throat. 'Are you free tonight? I'm playing Handel's oboe sonata. It will give you a marvellous introduction to the instrument. And then I could buy you dinner.'

She looked at him blankly.

'There is something between us,' he said. 'This morning,

when we were speaking, I could feel it.'

'I was interviewing you,' she said.

She went back to her typewriter and finished her report on the retiring postmaster. He was a lovely man. The editor declared it the article of the week and gave her R10. The paper ran eleven paragraphs on the oboe player the next day. There were very few mistakes.

Helen and the mountain

You need at least three sources to write a news report. I have not interviewed the others. I was not an eye witness.

This is not a news report. I do not need to begin by explaining who-what-where-when.

I could start with Jack, with the first time I met him. When the person introducing us said: 'Isn't Jack the sexiest man you've ever seen?' And I laughed, thinking it a joke, but Jack took it as his due.

Still, I'd rather start with Rosie.

Every day Rosie made an entrance in the *Chronicle* newsroom: late, wet hair, unpredictable garments. She chain-smoked at her desk beside mine and advised Carol on ways to revive her fiancé's libido. Across the room Helen typed steadily.

Rosie told me she was going to be a nurse. But she was caught in Fran's bed one night and – while no one could prove anything – she thought journalism might be a less restrictive career. Fran stayed on at the nursing college, qualified and on her weekends off drove three hours to visit Rosie. They made a striking couple, all legs, eyes and spiky hair. Men wouldn't leave them alone. Fran told them to fuck off, but Rosie kept them talking.

Most staff members worked on the *Chronicle* reluctantly. Rosie and I had failed to secure positions on better newspapers in more exciting cities. Jack and Jane had left interesting jobs at the coast to climb the corporate ladder: Jack was deputy editor,

Jane news editor. Only Carol, the crime reporter, and Helen, the court reporter, seemed content – they had always lived in this dull, conservative city and now that they both wore engagement rings it seemed they always would.

All the salaried staff on the *Chronicle* were white; black freelancers worked in a different room for a different edition called the *Chronicle Special*. All the reporters in the newsroom were women. All the photographers and sub-editors and editors were men; men who found excuses to come into the newsroom more frequently after Rosie joined the staff.

Rosie bashed out stories about stray dogs looking for homes on her heavy typewriter, grumbling about her wasted talent. Jane was a stern news editor. She had created an invisible wall between the reporters and her larger desk and dealt with Rosie's ideas for sensational exposés curtly. Rosie would go on a go-slow and call Carol over for another lesson in seduction involving fragrant showers and walking in front of TV sets clad only in a towel.

When the editor or deputy editor visited the newsroom, Rosie went up to him and begged to be assigned some hard-nosed investigative reporting. Jack intoned 'Rosie, Rosie' and said his years in small newsrooms had helped him become a prize-winning journalist. The editor laughed nervously and told Rosie the *Chronicle* wasn't a foot-in-the-door kind of paper.

It was hard to know what kind of paper the *Chronicle* was. A newspaper with a proud heritage, certainly, the oldest paper in the province. And a newspaper that was losing money – in a company that valued profits above all else. If the *Chronicle* wanted to survive it had to improve its sales and advertising. The editor believed this was best done with bland news. He liked stories about agriculture, unusual weather and escaped zoo animals. Political stories were written by the newspaper group's correspondents, who were based elsewhere but occasionally worked from the *Chronicle* newsroom.

When a chinless political correspondent took up temporary

residence at a spare desk one day, Rosie signalled to Carol. 'Observe the master at work,' she mouthed. Rosie was dressed as a schoolgirl that day: white shirt, checked skirt, white socks, high-heeled shoes with buckles. She clip-clopped across the newsroom and extended her hand and teeth to the correspondent. She returned to her desk with an invitation to join him for drinks to discuss her career path.

The following morning Carol perched on Rosie's desk and demanded a blow by blow. Rosie dwelt on the drinks drunk and the courses eaten and the exact way she had held her glass and fork and where she had touched her face and how often. I laughed, but Carol begged Rosie to fast forward and eventually she reached the end of the evening when she arrived back at her garden cottage with the political correspondent. She described how she had extricated herself from his arms by pouring two whiskies and suggesting a game of chess. The disappointed correspondent agreed, but halfway through Rosie announced that she had to shower – alone. She re-emerged in a bathrobe with a few tendrils of hair fetchingly damp and insisted they finish the match. Every time the correspondent seemed to be concentrating too hard, Rosie leaned forward to reveal a bit more cleavage, and in this way checkmated him easily. As a consolation prize she let him kiss her here and there, but as he was removing his trousers she confessed that she loved women.

Rosie spoke loud enough for the surrounding desks to hear. Even Helen laughed at the climax.

Helen was quiet and hardworking. She rarely joined us for evening drinks, rarely went to our weekend parties or picnics beside mud-coloured rivers. And when she did, she never brought her fiancé. Rosie went to every gathering and Fran came too when she was visiting.

It was soon after the political correspondent's visit that Jack announced a newsroom outing to climb Thaba Nchu. He had obtained a permit from the mountaineering club to sleep in a cave near the top of the mountain. Attendance was compulsory for all reporters and photographers, he said. There was grumbling. Carol did not possess one pair of walking shoes and could not afford to buy any. The chief photographer had a family wedding to attend. Jack said everybody else had to come. Rosie asked if she could bring Fran.

On Saturday morning we piled into three cars with backpacks, sleeping bags, sandwiches, firewood, braai meat and booze and drove east. It took an hour to reach the base of Thaba Nchu: the black mountain, the bald mountain. Jack was in schoolteacher mode, lecturing about King Moshoeshoe allowing Moroko's people to settle below the mountain. And how Thaba Nchu was a lookout spot during the Boer War. I looked at the arid land and village and tried to imagine a country without bantustans.

We parked beside a rusted fence and started to climb, the smokers at the back. Jack led the way. Rosie complained about the steep path as she chased after Fran. Helen and I walked doggedly. Jane chatted to the photographers. The air was crisp. The sky vast. And then we were at the top. And then we were in the cave unpacking our provisions while Jack poured whisky into plastic mugs and supervised the building of the campfire.

On Monday morning, after Rosie rushed in late – wet hair, white jeans – Carol padded over to her desk on stockinged feet. The newsroom was quiet. Helen's desk was empty. Jane was in the morning news conference with the editors. The photographers were developing negatives. The freelance reporters were in their separate room. I was shuffling through press releases for the weekly film guide, unable to concentrate.

Rosie borrowed Carol's cigarette to light her own and gesticulated angrily. 'If it had been anyone else,' she hissed furiously. 'Anyone but Helen. And you should have seen Jack the next morning. Swaggering. All puffed up. Nobody would speak to him but he didn't care. Helen left before breakfast, Jane went with her. The rest of us had to squash into two cars and no one wanted to drive with Jack.'

Carol turned to me for verification, but I shrugged. Whisky and fresh air had sent me to sleep straight after supper.

Carol asked questions and Rosie impatiently rattled off details: the delayed braai, the way Jack kept topping up the reporters' mugs, the circle of sleeping bags around the fire, the zipping and unzipping of sleeping bags. 'Everyone could hear Jack panting away,' Rosie said. 'And Helen had had so much to drink.'

Carol's eyes bulged. She put her hands on either side of Rosie's typewriter and leaned forward, speechless. Rosie looked up at her and then looked away. 'Let me give you some advice, Carol,' she said. 'Always keep your nose clean.'

Profile

Sally was painting silhouettes. She made us all stand against the wall, one at a time. She angled the reading lamp to produce a shadow of our profiles, sketched the outline in pencil and filled it in with paint. She used different colours, overlapped some heads. It was a mural; a record of our bunch of kibbutz volunteers. She captured Craig's aquiline nose, Maryke's taut jawline, Sarah's wild hair, Hiroki's sharp cheekbones. When it was my turn Sally tried one angle after another: profile from the left, profile from the right, a three-quarter view. All she got was a lopsided oval: short hair, flat forehead, full cheeks and a nose and chin that barely broke the contour. 'I can't do yours,' she said. 'There's nothing there.'

Baby dolls

Once upon a time before cell phones, in the City of Roses, Bernadette Cloke lived with her mother and father in a big house at the end of a long driveway lined with trees.

Her friends had all gone to universities far away but Bernadette was careful. She stayed home and studied through correspondence.

Every night at ten o'clock her mother gave her a vial of golden nectar and massaged her plump feet. Bernadette would sigh and say: 'How I would love a pair of cork platforms, or cowboy boots, or slip-slops.'

Every Saturday Mrs Cloke drove her daughter to town to buy a new pair of shoes. Bernadette could choose any style she liked. She had shelves and shelves of shoes. She had boxes and boxes of boots. But she only ever wore flat baby dolls in soft black fabric. She wore them with short white socks.

Now Bernadette was twenty-two. She was getting tired of being careful. She was getting tired of being good. She went to a pub and ordered wine. She accepted a smoke from a man at the bar. She let him make her laugh and wrote her phone number on his box of matches. She drove home in her silver Audi and was late for her golden vial.

'I'm not apologising,' she told her mother, as Mrs Cloke rubbed antiseptic cream into her toes. 'I met a dinky man called Timothy.'

Bernadette liked driving beside Timothy in his rusty Mini,

watching the tar through the holes in the chassis. She liked visiting him at The Plot where he rented a falling down house with a couple who rode Harley-Davidsons and collected LPs.

Mr Cloke said The Plot was a graveyard for dead cars and deadbeats. He said by the age of thirty a man should have more to his name than half a degree and a string of dead-end jobs.

Mrs Cloke said: 'Are you looking after yourself, love? Are you being careful?'

Bernadette said she was tired of eating nutritious meals with her parents three times a day. She was tired of having a mother who gave her a cooler-box with golden nectar whenever she left the house.

She liked the breakfast fry-ups and fiery curries they ate at The Plot with beer. She lay on the tatty carpet smoking Benson & Hedges Special Mild and making mixed tapes of Rolling Stones love songs. She learnt to play poker and drink whisky.

She liked sitting on the toilet seat while Timothy reclined in the bath with Gitanes and a quart. He looked vulnerable with wet hair. Her stomach hurt when he spoke about a woman he loved who was studying in America.

Bernadette was still careful. She showered alone, she remembered the golden nectar, she remembered her creams, she emerged in a long nightie and clean socks.

Timothy made her happy.

She didn't mind when their lovemaking ended with him cursing and vowing never to drink again. It was enough for her to wake up to his face. She wasn't scared of him after he smashed a few things, punched his fist through a pane of glass and sat down to write an inventory of what he'd broken. She was scared for him.

Things changed when Timothy lost his job.

Bernadette said of course she would drive with him to the coast.

Mr Cloke slammed doors and gave his daughter an open air-ticket home.

Mrs Cloke took Bernadette to town to look for shoes for the trip. The shop assistants fluttered around with boxes of takkies and padded clogs. Bernadette left wearing moccasins. By the time they were back home she was in tears. Mrs Cloke washed her daughter's throbbing feet and rubbed ointment into the fresh sores. Then she quietly unpacked a new pair of soft black shoes and wept as she handed her daughter a heavy cooler-bag.

I wish I could say Bernadette wore silver stilettos to her wedding and she and Timothy lived happily ever after.

But Bernadette wasn't careful in the tropical city.

She stayed up late drinking and listening to jazz and hearing how Timothy's father had gambled and drunk his money away.

She climbed over a high gate to see the thatched house Timothy grew up in, and bashed her foot when guard dogs chased them out again. She said nothing about her injury and was pleased when her toes went numb and the pain disappeared.

She tried not to bother Timothy's parents who seemed so unhappy in their tiny flat. She ignored her splitting headaches. She ignored her blurred vision. She fell asleep, for the last time, without showering or changing her socks.

Danger Point

Once a girl walked along a beach of white sand. She walked at sunset to the furthest rocks. She waited for the lighthouse. It flashed three times. Then paused. Then flashed three times.

She watched until it was nearly dark. If she'd been a ship she would have steered straight for it. Three flashes. Pause. Three flashes.

She tried to walk to the lighthouse once. She crossed two rivers before turning back.

Every time she walked along the beach she looked for him. When the currents were cold she expected him to loom out of the sea mist. She would know him when she saw him. He would be wearing an old jersey. He would be looking for her.

She brought men to the beach. Friends who spent hours fishing from the rocks. A lover who moaned about the wind, the stench of decaying kelp, the haze of sea lice.

One overcast day she drove to the lighthouse. After the second town she turned left and followed a sandy road. It led to an octagonal tower with four narrow windows running up four alternate sides. The tower supported a cage of glass topped with a red hat.

The keeper emerged from the arched front door. He told her the lighthouse was eighteen metres high, built of concrete blocks and mortar. A lens weighing twenty kilograms gave the rotating bulb the power of one million seven hundred thousand candles. The light flashed three times every forty seconds.

He said the lighthouse wasn't open to the public. He wouldn't let her inside. Security reasons. But he gave her a bulb. A giant clear globe. Its broken fuse vibrated.

3

I was wearing jeans

I heard someone on the radio say that the more you recall a memory, the more you change it. So if you ask me what I was wearing last Christmas Eve I might say jeans and a green shirt. But I might be wrong.

I know I wore jeans the Christmas Eve I was nineteen because I was groped. It's easy to grope a woman in a crowd. You put your hand deep down her right front pocket. While she tries to pull it out, you put your other hand into her left pocket and remove her cash. It happened to me in Bethlehem. I had joined hundreds of tourists in the square outside the Church of the Nativity. We were watching the Latin mass on a screen. I remember bodies pressing into me from behind and quick hard stick fingers wriggling down, burrowing in. It was over before I had time to scream. I remember feeling winded with surprise. I swung around and confronted a row of young faces all looking up at me blankly.

Four years later I was groped as a crowd pushed its way into a Port Elizabeth reggae concert. I remember the press of bodies as we surged through the door. I was probably wearing jeans because I remember the hand sliding in. It felt the same as the Bethlehem hand, as if the hand was following me. The same hard thin fingers. The same wriggling. I had the same instinct to fight, felt the same confusion afterwards.

I only had a bit of money in my pocket on both occasions. Not a big loss. Not a big violation. And on the El Al flight back to

South Africa an old man came up to me. I think he was old but maybe now I wouldn't think he was that old. I was in economy on the aisle with just enough space to place my camel leather bag between my hiking boots. The old man came up to me and said there was a free seat in first class. I have a hazy memory of his face when he said it. He seemed open, matter of fact, passing on information. And I thought, why not. I had heard about the extra space, the better food. I stood up in my jeans and white T-shirt and followed him through the dividing curtain and he showed me a spare seat next to his. I don't remember having a conversation with him, just that first class seemed hushed, my seat felt bigger. Then he slid his hand under my thigh and I went back to economy.

Another incident. Another flight. I was about twenty-six and had just returned to Joburg after visiting my family. I was probably wearing the pixie shoes I liked then – black, pointy lace-ups with bits of red and yellow leather sewn in at the sides. And black jeans and an emerald jersey. Or green jeans and a purple jersey. What can I say, it was the eighties.

I drove myself home to Yeoville from the airport, parked in the street outside Creighton Hall and carried my grey holdall into the unlocked foyer. There was a guy around my age. We were in the foyer together. He was wearing a jersey with a diamond pattern. He was near the lift. I was going to take the lift but then I thought I'd rather take the stairs because I didn't want that awkward being in the lift with one other person thing. I used to take two steps at a time. I was on my way up the stairs, which were covered with those beige speckled tiles with a few lines cut into them at the edge to provide traction. I was wearing jeans. I was wearing my pixie shoes with thin soles. I tap-tapped my way up the steps. I was halfway up the second flight of stairs when suddenly these fingers burrowed into me from behind. Big fingers pushing the seam of my jeans. Rough. I fell to my knees. A sound came out of my lungs: a breathless primal shriek I had never made before, and he ran away. I turned and caught a flash of his grey jersey as he disappeared around the corner.

I thought I saw the same man at a gallery opening a few months later. I was probably wearing my favourite going out clothes then: black and white striped leggings and a long black T-shirt. The man was in a patterned jersey. He caught me staring at him and looked away. He was gazing at another woman. She wore a leather bomber jacket and faded jeans which fell straight from her hips. Her thighs didn't announce themselves like mine did. I told my friend I thought the guy in the grey jersey had groped me. But I couldn't be sure. Lots of people wore those jerseys.

So that was all that happened to me. Nothing to write home about. Nothing to write about. I haven't been in therapy or studied psychology and my idea of history is sifting through boxes of papers at archives, not theorising. But the voice on the radio made sense: the more you remember something, the more you change the memory. So if I tell you I wore a multi-coloured dress last Christmas Eve I can see myself in it.

❖

I can't say what I wore the Christmas Eve I spent in Bloemfontein when I was twenty-three. I remember I wore a hessian jacket and a tie to work once and the deputy editor said: 'Who is this young man?' I still wanted to dress like a student then and on the weekends I wore denim dungarees with a yellow vest.

I invited the deputy editor and his girlfriend for supper when I moved into my first flat on the edge of town. It was a bachelor flat in Fort Drury Mansions, a sprawling complex built in the 1930s with thick walls and arches. My flat was tiny. It was long and thin with a mattress on the floor at one end and a kitchenette under a window at the other. I bought metres of bright cotton – red and purple with striped borders in different colours – and I made a bedspread out of it and taped another length to the wall. I had a rubber plant in a pot and a couple of ornaments and a three-in-one slow-cooker my mother gave me. I made a Moroccan dish with zucchini and yoghurt and left it to simmer all day and served it to my guests. The next day the deputy editor told me he'd had diarrhoea and blamed my cooking. I laughed and didn't believe him because I was fine.

I only stayed in that flat for a month or two, before I moved to Port Elizabeth. I only met one other Fort Drury resident, a junior lecturer in sociology. We had some mutual friends and I went around to his flat a few times, probably after I'd been working night duty. His flat was larger than mine with a separate bedroom and a lounge with couches and a coffee table and shelves overflowing with books. The lecturer had long dark hair which fell into his eyes. He wore jeans and tweed jackets. He gave me a drink and asked if I wanted to go for a walk and we strode around the empty city centre until midnight. We walked past my office and I took him to see the printing press in action.

The lecturer spoke about his lover, who was married with children and wanted to end their affair. He played music I didn't know and we drank wine and smoked grass. The last time I visited him must have been just before I left for Port Elizabeth. I remember sitting on the floor next to his coffee table, books and papers strewn around. He showed me photographs of his lover, large glossy black and white photographs of them together. She had long slim legs, long blonde hair cut in the shaggy style that was fashionable then and a face to match.

I remember I was sitting on the carpet at the coffee table and I was feeling a bit drunk and stoned and lumpy compared to his movie star lover. And he was sitting in a chair and he held up a pill and said, 'I got this from someone, I don't know what it does but if you like we can share it.' And I said sure or okay or why not or something. And I remember waking up in his lounge the next morning and he wasn't in the room, and walking home and going back to sleep. Sleeping all day.

Then I remembered waking up and noticing that my

dungaree strap had come undone and feeling embarrassed about that. The memory came back clearly and I could see myself waking up when it was already morning, and quickly hooking the clasp back over the metal button of my dungarees before I let myself out. And I could feel myself feeling woozy, looking around and not seeing him in the room, looking for the door, which was unlocked, and going out.

And then I had this feeling that I'd been embarrassed. Embarrassed about falling asleep and embarrassed about something else.

The more I thought about it the more I remembered feeling uncomfortable in another way. Walking back home and feeling like something wasn't right. Sitting on the toilet with my dungarees bunched around my knees and feeling sore. Feeling groggy and going to sleep for the whole day and whole night and feeling fine again.

Or am I imagining it?

But I can feel myself waking up, disorientated, dried spit at the side of my mouth, embarrassed that my dungarees had come undone. Embarrassed that I had passed out in his flat. A sore scratchy feeling I wasn't used to as I stumbled the short way home. I can see myself sitting on the toilet. See the dungarees in a heap around my feet. I don't know what shoes I was wearing. Maybe leather sandals.

But I know I was wearing a black dress with a diamond pattern last Christmas Eve; my sister-in-law sent me a photograph.

Riptide

This is about a man in a doorway. A tall man in army uniform who looked too big, or his uniform looked too small. An army man who took off his beret and smiled until his eyes crinkled. I smiled back. And we were glad we had finally met because there were only five people in that city who thought like us. One of them was his wife, and I worked with his wife.

This is about desire but it needn't have been if his wife hadn't left town. If she hadn't returned to the coast and moved into a house with my sister. If the army man and I hadn't driven down together to visit them one weekend. If we hadn't loved the same music. If we hadn't had so much to speak about. And it wasn't just about the war. It wasn't just about conscription. It wasn't just about how he felt wearing that uniform.

This is about half glances and drinking looks and undercurrents and cross-currents and a floating feeling when we first arrived at the coast. That night I shared a bed with my sister and we smoked grass. In the morning I passed the bedroom of the army man and his wife. I didn't look through the open door. I only glanced, but it was enough to see them sleeping naked on the sheet.

But believe me I did not pursue this man. Except when we were back in the city he phoned and I answered. He said he was leaving for good and was there somewhere nice to go for a meal. I said the place with glasses like vases. He asked would I come. And it was just us two. We drank. Afterwards we were in my flat and we kissed.

And believe me I said, what about your wife. And he said, she doesn't need to know. Maybe those weren't his exact words but that's what I remember. That's what I understood. He said we have an open relationship. And I smiled because we all believed that open relationships were good. All of us who saw things differently in that city, who believed in freedom and equality and mistrusted the bourgeois institution of marriage. People who thought like us only married so their lovers could visit them in prison or give them a foreign passport. And the army man said he had only married so he could live outside the barracks. And I believed him.

But I didn't pursue him. I didn't arrange to meet him the next day. And I don't remember how we ended up at the same time at a place with a few shops and a restaurant. He said let me buy you lunch. I let him. The restaurant wasn't too big, or too small. The light was dim.

And this is a story about desire and we were both drunk with it.

Later that same afternoon my friends phoned and said come for supper. They said it was to say goodbye to the army man. I went. After supper the army man and I went outside to our cars. We didn't leave. We didn't switch on the engines. He came over to my window and said would you like to go for a walk, even though there was nowhere to walk. It was just a smallholding. But there was a stable.

So we walked along dirt tracks that cut through dead grass to the stable. There was a moon but the street lights turned everything the same flat orange. The stable was rank, the horse long gone, so we kept the door open. There was no manger, there was no lying down. So he knelt. So we stood.

And believe me I didn't phone the army man after he left town. But I might have sent a letter. I might have sent a letter via my sister. Perhaps I told him I was going to a party in another place because he was at this party. He was alone. And we were with people who thought like us – many more than five. They asked about his wife and he smiled and said that she was fine.

And I remember I was wearing a summer dress that was blue and white over the breasts and white and blue below. And I had tied an Indian scarf around my waist. And in the morning I was dressed just the same. We hadn't slept at all. And we did things. Things I had done before and would do again and would enjoy as much, or more. But it was as if I did them with him first.

Believe me when I say I can't remember when I wrote the letter. Whether it was after we drove to my sister or after the stable or after the party. And I wasn't trying to change his life. I wasn't asking to have him all for myself. I was trying to tell him how I felt. How I felt pulled. How I felt tugged. How I felt drawn. Or that is how I remember it.

And it was late one night when his wife called and screamed at me. I was asleep when she phoned. I was at home, in my bed and I held the phone close to my ear as she screamed and said what right did I have. What right did I have to write those things to her husband. And I listened.

I never contacted him again. I moved on. I met someone else and then someone else and then someone else and then someone I never wanted to say goodbye to.

And it was then that the army man phoned. Of course he was no longer an army man. And he was no longer married. When I didn't return his calls he arrived at my office. He stood in the doorway. A tall man whose thinning hair had grown, whose jeans fitted. And how could I not join him for coffee.

But believe me I didn't speak about the tugging, the pull. I didn't speak about the riptide that sucked us in deep and spat us out. And I still believed the war was evil. I still believed the revolution was good. But I didn't believe in open relationships. And I had met someone I couldn't say goodbye to. So I looked away. I watched the cups, the coffee cups on the conveyor belt, going round and round. I looked away. I only glanced at his eyes, his hands, his mouth.

Carousel

It was the men walking towards me. It was my split-open bag. It was the way one man held it away from him as if it stank. I was alone at the airport carousel. No more bags coming out of its mouth of plastic sheets. No people leaning over to grab their suitcases.

It was a stupid thing to do. To put the books in that flimsy bag. A shopping bag that folded up into a wallet. My mother gave it to me at the last moment. I packed in a rush. I had to have one more swim in the sea. I had to buy all those books. I needed enough for a year. I bought *Time Longer Than Rope: The Black Man's Struggle in South Africa* and *The Second Sex* and *The Selected Works of Marx and Engels*. I bought *Freud for Beginners* and *Really Bad News*, which both had comics, and *The Truth About Afghanistan* with minuscule text straight from the Soviet Union. I bought too many for hand luggage.

It was how I pictured myself in that inland city, alone at night reading, making notes, pausing to light another cigarette. It was a lie. Smoking made me sick. I spent my evenings drinking with colleagues. My weekends too.

It was my instinct to run. I was frozen. It was my practice to keep quiet if I had nothing to say. If the questions were rhetorical. What are you doing with all these books? I was first born. I was raised to please. I was raised to obey my parents, my teachers. I was raised to see the government as evil.

It was easier to go with the men. I was taken to a small room.

I signed a piece of paper with a list of books. I waited while phone calls were made. I was given all my books but one: *Time Longer Than Rope* with Sharpeville on its cover – policemen standing, bodies lying, red sun rising, red banner shouting *BANNED in South Africa*. I had instructions to report to the security police.

It was possible my housemates' phone was bugged. I drove to a tickey-box, reversed charges. My mother sounded angry. My liberal mother said: What are you really up to? What are you involved in? Rhetorical questions. My father called a lawyer.

It was unavoidable, the visit to the security police. The lawyer and my editor both said so. I went alone to a vast slab of brick and concrete, iron and steel. Through gates and gates and gates all unlocked and relocked. The colonel was a surprise. He smiled. He had my father's square face, similar spectacles. He said my book was banned for distribution, not possession. He gave it back. He asked could he phone me from time to time at the newspaper. I shook my head. He said don't answer now.

It was easy to say no on the phone. It was easy to say no at my next job when an American voice asked me for background information. I told him everything I knew was in my press reports. I knew about the CIA, how they were in cahoots with the government. I knew about the security police spy in every newsroom. I knew it was the security police who stabbed my car tyres and sent a note: *Die you commie bastard*. Things were black and white and white was bad.

It was because I was white that the small-town hotel gave me a good room. It was because he was not that the advocate was turned away. The hotel owner told me it was because there were no rooms available with private bathrooms. The advocate told me he wouldn't have minded sharing. After my front page story he got an en suite room.

It was a series of court cases. They went on for months. There were charges of public violence, assault, intimidation and malicious damage to property. There were convictions for stoning funeral processions and assaulting teachers. The minors got five to seven cuts with a light cane. The adults were sent to prison for two to six years. There were allegations about police beating confessions out of schoolchildren. There was a magistrate who said the reasons behind the protests didn't concern the court; what was important was that order was restored in the community.

It was a clear divide. The state structures on one side, the new civic and youth organisations on the other. The children had been boycotting school for a year. They wanted to elect student leaders. They wanted their headmaster reinstated. The headmaster who also chaired the civic organisation. The police did their best to eradicate resistance. The community did its best to make state employees feel unsafe, they wanted township policemen, teachers and councillors to resign and join their cause.

It was as if I was recording history. I was the only reporter in town. I sat through every word of those trials. I filled notebooks. I returned to my hotel room and bashed out stories on my typewriter. I called the newsroom from the lobby and dictated my reports. I had supper with the advocate in the dining room. He ordered whisky, I drank white wine.

It was a victory of sorts for the defence. More trialists were acquitted than sent to jail. The security policemen who sat behind the state prosecutor didn't look happy. Neither did the prosecutor. The prosecutor didn't like my press reports. The way I recorded every allegation of police brutality. The way I quoted the advocate more than him.

It was the last day of the last trial. My last evening in the hotel. My room was on the ground floor. It had glass doors. The curtains were open. I had typed and dictated my final report. My typewriter was zipped into its case. My cassette tapes were in a box. I had packed my clothes. I was packing my notebooks and novels – Marge Piercy's *Vida*, about sex and activism, and George Orwell's *1984* because that was the year.

It was a young policeman who knocked on the glass door. He had an accent like my first boyfriend who said fush instead of fish. The policeman invited me to a braai. It was a tradition, he said, at the end of a long trial. Everyone was coming. He had come to give me a lift.

It was the least I could do, I thought. I had taken sides. Silently I had cheered each defence victory, grudged the state each conviction it secured. The magistrate was hosting the braai, the policeman said. He had invited the advocate and prosecutor. The policeman teased me. He made me laugh. He said it would be rude of me to refuse.

It was because he had an early morning flight that he probably wouldn't make the braai, the advocate said, when we passed him in the lobby. I hesitated. The policeman ushered me into his van and drove me out of town. We stopped at a few outbuildings, a concrete dam, a small group of men braaiing meat in a half-drum. The magistrate looked embarrassed, downed his drink and left.

It was a choice between brandy or beer or wine, the smiling prosecutor said. A security policeman poured wine into a glass. The prosecutor gave me a paper plate with a chop and boerewors. One security policeman put his arm around me. The other took a photograph.

Fallacies

You must choose whom to betray.

You are in a hotel suite with a four-poster bed. Your attorney and advocate have suites down the corridor. You knock on the advocate's door after supper. He says: *Follow your conscience.*

Your conscience says one thing. The state's laws another.

You worry that the suites are bugged. That this is the reason you were upgraded. You lie in your vast bed at night. Alone. Awake.

You must choose which lover to betray.
A or B.

You meet A on your first night in the windy city.

You arrive in the dark, leaves and grit and litter swirling. You park outside M's flat in the city centre, cross the chequered tiles in the entrance foyer, climb the steps to her floor. M works on the newspaper you are joining. She gives you food and wine. She tells you where to rent a flat, where to buy coffee, who to trust in the newsroom.

A arrives after supper. Unexpectedly. M has two beds in her spare room. The wind hammers the sash window. *Are you still awake,* you ask A.

You have another night with A. You throw a flat-warming party in your building near M's. Everyone dances to mixed tapes. Everyone leaves. Then A returns and puts his arms around you.

A is a student but he spends all his time working for the voteless. He asks you to write a document to help rural people understand how newspapers work. You can deny him nothing. A lives in another city. You rarely see him but when you do there is something between you. Something light and uncomplicated. Something which has run its course.

B is different.

B is a friend, a colleague. You know him from university. He calls you up one night and asks whether he should apply for a job in the windy city. You say: *Come.* When B tells your story he says: *She crashed her car, I crashed in her bed.* It's true. You call him the night of your crash. You don't want to be alone.

B is a reporter like you. A reporter on a different paper. You write with restraint, you win an award. B writes with passion, his reports are slashed by half.

B holds your face between his palms and says: *You are beautiful to me.* He writes you poems *dear milk-bottle legs, a pint of cream on the shiny side please.* He takes photographs of you next to a barbed-wire fence in the sunset. He tells you your document for A is too general and adds a critique on individual editors.

You must choose which contact to betray.

X or Y.

X is old and frail.

Y is dead.

X gives you stories for your newspaper. He keeps you up to date with what is happening in his township where police patrol neglected streets in armoured vehicles. Where children boycott schools and adults boycott rent increases.

X is the community spokesman there. He calls you when Y and his comrades are arrested and detained without trial. He calls when they are released many months later. X tells you they are freed but banned. They are listed: Y and his comrades cannot be quoted; their words cannot appear in print. X calls you after Y disappears. He calls with funeral arrangements after Y's stabbed and burnt body is found. He says everyone knows the police killed him and his comrades.

You are in this hotel suite because of a newspaper report you wrote. A report you wrote several months before Y was murdered.

Y's killers are free.

Y's killers are *persons unknown*.

You are on trial for writing untruths about the police. For reporting that they fired teargas into a church during a Sunday service.

You have witnesses who say they rushed out of the church with streaming eyes and coughing lungs. You have witnesses who say the police were furious because a policeman had been murdered earlier that day. You have the testimony of a church elder. You have the testimony of X.

The police have the evidence of policemen who say they were trying to disperse an angry mob. A crowd angry because a student leader had been arrested for the policeman's murder. The police regretted that the teargas canisters landed just outside the church building. They apologised to the church warden.

You have a memory of the night X calls to tell you about the church teargassing.

You hear his slow pedantic voice. You hear his voice asking questions, double-checking. You hear Y's voice in the background. You hear Y's impatience with your slow exchange. You hear X hand the telephone to Y. Y's voice on the line saying: *This is X*. Your voice saying: *Hello X*. Y speaking fast, fluently, hurrying you through the scenario. Y who is banned, listed, may not be quoted.

You must choose whom to betray.

You must decide whether to admit Y was your informant about the church teargassing.

X's credibility is in question. He has been charged with disability insurance fraud. A trumped-up charge, X says. But the prosecutor calls him untrustworthy.

If you betray Y you cannot hurt him. He is already smashed, knifed, torched.

If you betray Y you will hurt yourself. You will be put on trial for quoting a banned person.

If you betray Y then X will be charged with perjury: in his testimony X did not mention passing the phone to Y.

You are in the dock of a magistrate's court in the windy city.

You are on trial for writing untruths about the police.

You are on trial even though the allegations about the church teargassing were put to the police at the time. Even though your newspaper published the police spokesman's response.

You are on trial even though you are no longer employed by this newspaper – although they are paying for your defence; although the editor is charged alongside you.

You are working for another newspaper in another place because you were fired from your job in the windy city. You were fired after the security police showed your editor the document about dealing with the press. Your editor believed you were the author because of its critique of him and other editors. Because the critique contained information the editor had told you himself.

You must choose which lover to betray.

A has left the country.

B is a freelance reporter in the windy city. He reports on your trial from time to time.

B arrives as you are sitting outside the courtroom during an adjournment. You are no longer lovers but there is something between you. Something unresolved.

You tell B you know the prosecutor will question you about the document. Can you tell the court that B contributed to the document? That he supplied the critique on the editors?

B says: *No.*

B says: *Please, no.*

B was detained for three months. He was threatened with death. He is scared, vulnerable. He is a freelancer with no newspaper to back him.

You are in the witness box.

You are giving evidence in your defence.

You do not name Y.

You do not confess that you spoke to Y that night. You can tell the prosecutor knows you did. You can see his tight jaw, his tight fists. You know Y's phone was tapped. You know yours was. You could hear the click as the tape recorders switched on. You fear your hotel rooms are bugged too.

You are not brazen.

You do not find it easy to lie.

The magistrate can see your lowered eyelids, your flushed face. The magistrate will find you guilty. He will find your editor guilty too. The magistrate will impose fines and suspended sentences. He will reprimand you for not being an objective reporter. For choosing sides. For considering it your duty to expose police brutality. For considering it your duty to take the side of the oppressed.

You are not brazen.

You cannot lie twice. Not twice in a row.

The prosecutor does not spare you.

He asks about your friends in the windy city. He does not

ask about M, who left long before you. He asks about your friends who run literacy programmes and campaign against conscription. He asks about their whereabouts. He looks at the magistrate when you answer. When you say they are currently in prison, arrested under the State of Emergency, detained without trial.

The prosecutor holds up your document about dealing with the press.

He asks who requested you write it.

You give A's name.

The prosecutor asks if you know about A's senior position in the political front. He looks at the magistrate when you confirm that you do.

The prosecutor asks who else worked on the document.

He smiles when you ask the magistrate if you have to answer this question.

He smiles when the magistrate says that you do.

He smiles when you give B's name.

Tongue-tied

I didn't remember meeting him. I hardly looked at him in the bar. It was Ingrid who leaned towards his lighter with a fresh cigarette. Ingrid who insisted I go with her to meet him. I hadn't said much, hadn't stayed long. I had a boyfriend. I had an address book full of contacts I wasn't sharing with a stranger.

Another year, a bigger city, this stranger walks towards me on a soccer field filled with mourners. This stranger looks straight at me, hello again, playfully clipping my shoulder with his as he passes by with a camera crew. Casually sending a volt of light through me. There is a photograph of me taken that day, taken by accident. A photographer was developing a roll of film and there I am in the crowd toyi-toying to the graveyard. A crowd of mourners on their way to bury the mourners shot by police at the previous week's funeral. I look calm in the crowd. I look safe. I look like I'm thinking about someone's shoulder.

I might have forgotten the stranger if he hadn't phoned a week later. I worked for a foreign correspondent in the bigger city. The police telexed through a daily 'unrest' report listing the number of people shot and arrested. I rewrote these reports, replacing 'angry mobs' and 'riots' with 'protesters' and 'uprisings'. The correspondent said foreign readers needed perspective. I explained the geography of apartheid: the separation between white and black living areas – the lack of houses, water and electricity in the latter. The fact that most South Africans did not have the vote. I referred to the unofficial calendar observed by the protesters: the anniversaries of police massacres. Old massacres in Sharpeville and Soweto. New massacres in the Vaal Triangle and Uitenhage.

I didn't recognise the stranger's voice on the phone. I couldn't picture his face. I had hardly looked at him at the funeral. He had to mention mutual friends at the tiny newspaper where I worked in the afternoons. He had to mention Ingrid. It was his voice I listened to, not what he was saying. I couldn't work out the tone, why he was calling. He had to repeat that he wanted to ask me something. He wanted to talk over dinner.

I was expecting a knock on the door but there was a hoot. Then another hoot. I looked over my flat's balcony and saw a German car. I saw the man at the wheel lift his hand. I went downstairs, opened the passenger door, saw the leather seats. We drove to a restaurant that was once a church: a domed ceiling, starched tablecloths, celestial wine. He suggested I should order the pie but I chose fish and a salad. He asked why I had left Ingrid's city. I tried to explain but I couldn't remember to breathe. I couldn't swallow my food. I couldn't decide which parts of my story to emphasise. Which lovers to include, which colleagues, which activists. He listened and said he thought it was something like that. He seemed disappointed. He kissed me after he stopped outside my flat. He leaned across to open my car door from the inside, his mouth suddenly on mine.

Katherine knew the full story of why I left Ingrid's city. Katherine the newspaper unionist. She called me after I lost my job. She got the union to pay for my flight to the bigger city, appointed a lawyer to contest my unfair dismissal. We settled out of court. I got a letter of reference.

Ingrid had been my union representative in her city. She sat next to me when the editor fired me. She was there when my colleagues called a meeting to chastise me for choosing sides. Ingrid kept quiet. We lost touch after I moved to Katherine's city. It was Katherine who introduced me to the tiny newspaper where I worked in the afternoons, who took me to her parents for dinner.

I took my parents to the restaurant that was once a church, when they came to visit. I suggested they order the pie. I gave them my bed, kissed them goodnight and checked my answering machine. A message from Katherine, a spontaneous gathering to welcome her newborn daughter. I drove up the hill to her block of flats.

I was locking my car door when I looked up. Katherine lived in a tall face-brick slab but this building was sculptural. He was leaning over a curved balcony. Leaning, smoking a cigarette, smiling down. I asked should I come up and he buzzed me in. I climbed the stairs to the flat with the open door.

I liked conversation. I liked people who made me laugh. People who were clever and witty. He hardly spoke. He didn't try. I couldn't speak. We sat in his lounge then he stood up and left the room and came back and sat down again. He looked at me. I looked at him. I said something about his ear. It was a nice ear, flat against his skull. His eyes seemed lined with kohl. He tilted his head and gave me his ear.

You might say he was using me. I never knew when he would call. We usually went for dinner with other people – his work colleagues, his friends. He rarely sat next to me.

You might say I was using him. I never paid for anything. I barely spoke. I offered no opinions, never made him laugh. I was just waiting for the evening to be over and us to be alone in his room.

Sometimes other women had been in his flat before me. Once the coffee table was strewn with streamers, balloons and party hats. It was his birthday, he said, one corner of his mouth lifting. A friend had come around to cheer him up. Once I was in his lounge with other people. I spoke to them while I watched him. I watched how a husband played with his wife's hair, how he lifted her heavy hair with two hands and let it fall, then he stroked it. She closed her eyes like a cat.

I wrote a poem called occasional lovers. I was grown up. I wasn't needy. I wrote my news reports for foreign papers. I wrote features for the tiny newspaper. I snuck into a township hospital at night, saw the psychiatric patients strapped to their beds, the critically ill on blankets on the floor. I saw the uncollected urine samples, the pile of faeces on one bed, the blood and urine spills. I spoke to nurses and doctors in the overflowing wards. Nurses who also had to clean floors and serve food. Doctors with sleepless eyes who had to learn not to care. I typed the words. I had my work.

I had to leave a party. He was sitting on the floor across the room talking to my colleague, their heads close together, her hand on his knee. I asked her about him a few weeks later. She laughed. She said this calls for whisky. We closed the door of the tiny conference room and she filled two tumblers. She said there was nothing between them, they were just friends, they just fucked.

If I had to use one word to describe him, I would choose 'kind'. My body changed in his room, my skin turned taught and bronze.

Our longest conversations were about other women. There was a waitress in another city who gave him her phone number. She kept paging him while we ate pasta and he had to leave our table to use the restaurant's phone. There was a woman who loved another man more than him. He took this woman away on holidays. Then he would get back and phone me and I would say how was your trip.

I was at his next birthday party. I bought him an LP. I wrapped it and left it in my car. I arrived at the club as a stripper pulled him onto the stage. I could see him talking to her as she perched on his knee. They left the stage hand in hand. I felt sick with envy. Afterwards everyone spoke about how he had told the stripper not to undress further and not to undress him and not to do all the things he knew she had been paid to do. The women at the party praised him for how well he had handled the situation. They lambasted the jerks who had ordered the stripper. The woman he took on holidays wasn't at that party. My colleague left early, it was a week night. I stayed until I got a chance to speak to him. I said I had a present. He seemed pleased, then his friends led him away. I never gave him the LP, but I listened to it a lot.

He called me the night I heard my ex-boyfriend had been detained. I spent the night. In the morning he asked what was wrong.

He called when I had a new boyfriend. He asked me to a function. He said wear a ball gown. He said a mutual friend would be sorry I had declined.

I saw him at a premiere. A film about families searching for relatives detained without trial. He was seated on the aisle and he took my arm as my new boyfriend and I walked by. He held onto my arm and pulled me down towards him, kissed me hello. I followed my boyfriend to our seats. We watched the film. Me and my arm, my electric arm.

Amnesia

She loses the words she writes down. They travel from head to hand and fall from her fingers. She is a gardener sweeping up the words that mouths release, raking up the sentences of lawyers and academics. She collects a pile of words and sentences then chooses just a few to display. Once they have been planted in print they leave her.

Decades later she finds her reports on a civil conflict, reads them as if for the first time.

We were in our yard when we saw the group coming.
We went inside but they broke the windows and climbed
inside. They stabbed me three times, on my back, then
they threw stones at my wife. They chopped our hands
with a bush knife. Later that night our five-roomed house
was burnt down. Our younger sons took the dogs but we
don't know what happened to our pigeons.

She remembers her week in that small city. She stayed in a hotel at one end of the street. The Supreme Court was at the other end.

This is what we lost in the fire or have left behind:
A truckload of sand and 12 bags of cement to plaster
the house.
Furniture.
A fridge.

A hi-fi.
An orchard which produced oranges, naartjies,
peaches, pears, loquats, grapes, lemons, apples and
sugar cane.
A vegetable patch which yielded mealies, potatoes,
sweet potatoes and pumpkins.

The conflict was between an ethnic political party and the new civic front. The front claimed the ethnic party had the active support of the state: their warlords were known to the police but remained free. The civic front brought interdict after interdict against the warlords. But no one was arrested. The warlords remained at large. The conflict raged on.

We had two rondavels and a seven-roomed house of
concrete bricks. It was not yet completed. We were
just about to put the roof on. The children ask about
our three cows, 28 chickens and three dogs. More
than anything the older ones want to go back to their
school.

She has a vague memory of interviewing refugees in suburban servants' quarters. Her newspaper report says she also interviewed a woman hiding in a church room:

My 70-year-old father was murdered. This
happened after he brought an application against
warlords who threatened him because my brother
supported the civic front. My father's murderers
were the same men he named in his affidavit. They
stabbed him to death. They stabbed me twice. The
police have arrested no one.

She remembers driving out of town. The hills green and dotted with homesteads. Her report has a photograph of a warlord she interviewed. He denied calling for violence at a public meeting. He said members of the civic front had attacked leaders of his ethnic party first:

The police were, however, able to protect us and we reached home safely.

She remembers spending days sifting through affidavits collected by religious groups and human rights lawyers. Her reports contain the names of people she interviewed. She can't recall their faces. She can't recall writing the words she wrote.

She remembers what she didn't write down.

Her first night in the city. She phones the brother of a childhood friend. A tall measured man. They speak haltingly over dinner about their jobs and relationships. They sit side by side in a movie theatre while an actress boils her lover's pet rabbit. They part quickly afterwards.

Her last night in the city. Her hot humid hotel room. A ringing phone. A human rights lawyer saying come for supper. She has already eaten. A ringing phone. A lawyer listing the reasons why she should join him and another journalist and another lawyer. A restaurant in an old colonial building. Laughter.

Peripheral

She pays attention but she doesn't see. She has an astigmatism her contact lenses don't correct. She can't use her camera properly, can't see well enough to align the split screen or clear the dark microprism ring. It is hit and miss whether her photographs are in focus. It is hit and miss whether they are well composed.

A photograph of hers appears in a Washington newspaper. Teenagers at a mass township funeral to bury police victims. The teenagers wear khaki clothes and black berets; they carry wooden machine guns with AK-47 painted on the barrels. A photographer discusses composition with her, points out why her photograph works: the way the head of one teenager is higher than the rest, the way his raised hand points to the left and the teenager with the gun faces right. She knows it was a fluke. She has seen her negatives, the contact sheet, the strip of blurred photographs on either side.

She has tunnel vision. She sees what is in front of her. She wears her glasses if she works at home at night, finishing the feature articles she started in the day. She needs quiet to think, to focus. She concentrates on what occurred, not what was felt. She turns her head to see when she wears spectacles, the periphery is blurred, discounted.

She sees only what is in front of her. She looks into the eyes of the reporters who are her friends or trusted acquaintances. She looks away from the reporters believed to be working for the police.

When she arrives in a new city a colleague shows her around the townships. She concentrates on the grid of streets, the famous landmarks and houses, the hospital with prefab bungalows. Her guide's reluctance is peripheral, his discomfort at showing her around as if she were a foreigner.

She sees herself as a voice for the voteless. She doesn't focus on the voteless reporters assigned to cover sport or employed only as freelancers. She doesn't ask why the voteless reporter who covered the rent boycotts before her was taken off the beat.

She changes quotes so the voteless speak standard English, because she cannot interview people in their mother tongues. She doesn't see she is ignoring the way English is changing, that she is casually eclipsing voices herself.

Caged

I walked to the Carlton Centre at lunch time, took the escalators to the health shop in the basement, ordered chamomile tea and a salad with sprouts. I walked as much as I could to be part of the throng, the urgency. On Fridays, when the news conference started late in the morning, I walked from Yeoville to Marshalltown, via Berea and Doornfontein. If I was covering a trial I walked to the Supreme Court. It was magnetic – the dome, the wood-panelled courtrooms, the politely vicious battles between counsel for the defence and state.

You drove to the zoo for your lunch breaks. Caged animals were better than none. On Sundays you drove to nature reserves. You expanded with the space, the birdsong.

For our first date you took me to the cricket. You took my hand as we crossed the road, dropped it when we reached the pavement. You bought pies. I didn't eat pies, didn't watch sport, didn't want to break the sports boycott. I sat close to you and watched the spectators.

You took me to Black Sabbath. I didn't like heavy metal, didn't approve of Sun City, didn't want to break the cultural boycott. I borrowed ear plugs and slept on your shoulder.

For our first weekend away we camped at the Pilanesberg. We drove northwest from the city, through Rustenburg, past Bophuthatswana's endless labour camps. I looked for desolation in the apartheid-engineered poverty but all I saw were people in love. Young couples leaning towards each other, smiling as they walked.

Other mothers

The mentor's wife

His wife was beautiful, but older. She bustled in while they were working – to fetch a cup or do some filing – and checked the electricity. She looked through the window after collecting the post. Nothing. No charge between them: her husband and the young reporter he had rescued. The one who had been fired, who claimed she had been unfairly accused of bias. He understood. He too had been fired and falsely accused of incompetence. Two wounded castoffs cut off from the glory and madness of their newsrooms, they went freelance.

The mentor's wife was kind to the reporter. She lent her a towel and clean underwear after she worked through the night. The young one had been hired to help the mentor. But she didn't see or hear the way he did, so he worked just as hard. He set her up with foreign newspapers but she preferred to write for a struggling local rag. He introduced her to foreign correspondents but she fell for a sport-loving artist.

From the mentor the young one learnt that reporters should always drink or eat what people offer, because that is when they will relax and speak freely. And that a story is like a washing line, only washing belongs on it, nothing extraneous. From his wife she learnt how to cook with wine in a clay oven, how to add mustard to salad dressing, how to sleep all night on a hard floor next to an asthmatic son.

The widow

She didn't cry at their funeral. Her face shone, her fist cut the air before the coffins draped in flags, men in black berets carrying banners, the defiant multitude. The army and police watched from the perimeter, for one day only.

I met her a year before. She was already in mourning. Her husband in prison, detained without trial. She wore a dressing gown. Her daughter leaned against her arm. Her son snuggled against her breast. She stroked his hair with her fingers, covered his plump forehead with the palm of her hand. Her dressing gown was belted tight.

The stalwart

The last time I saw her we had tea overlooking her garden. She might have smoked a cigarette. We must have discussed my research, which she had commissioned. I told her I was leaving the city soon; my boyfriend wanted to be a game ranger. Let me give you some advice, she said.

I waited for this stalwart with her muscular mind to say the things I was ignoring. What about your career? Are you going to give up your dreams to follow a man? Can we call you if we hear of human rights abuses there? At least keep a journal. But she looked at me and said: Look after your skin. Wear sunscreen every day.

4

Separate schedules

Doep shaved a patch of hair off your arm. He used his knife, his bush knife. You didn't flinch. You didn't object.

We came to work at the game lodge because you wanted to see a leopard. Because you juggled lemons in our kitchen in the city. You kept your eyes on the lemons in the air and asked: 'Will you be my fiancée?' I said that wasn't the way to ask the question.

You always say we never made love at the game lodge. I remember having sex. Having sex like strangers. You were a stranger to me then with your short hair, your short-sleeved khaki shirt, your tight shorts, your tight face. All I recognised were your woolly arms and legs.

Doep and Burt bought you drinks on our first night at the lodge. They leaned against the bar counter and watched how you held your liquor. They cross-examined you about elephants and blue waxbills. They questioned the relevance of your bird books, the strength of your binoculars. They were irritated when you wouldn't talk about your army experiences. They sniggered because you didn't have a knife. Doep produced his. He held it close to your face for you to admire. He left a bald patch on your forearm.

We got our jobs at the lodge because of me. Many men wanted to be rangers. Many men wanted to drive Land Rovers through dry river beds looking for cheetah and wild dogs. Not as many women wanted to work as housekeepers and receptionists. Not that many women reminded the lodge's manager of an old girlfriend.

I was not accustomed to being around men with knives and rifles.

I was accustomed to spending hours in the state archives. To sifting through Native Affairs Department documents from the 1940s, when black subsistence farmers revolted against laws controlling how and where they farmed. To sifting through papers for the voices of the voteless: *they all stated that the land belongs to them and they could plough where they liked and as much as they liked … the land belongs to them and their grandfathers and they can do what they like.*

The subsistence farmers' revolt was north of the city where we lived. The game lodge was to the east. The lodge bordered a huge national park. A park where people who had lived and hunted for generations were evicted to make space for animals; where some were forced to set fire to their own dwellings before leaving.

I was fine for a few months at the lodge.

I was fine in the summer.

I worked in reception, the doors were open, the thatched roof kept everything cool. When the rangers and foreign tourists left for their evening game drive I was off duty. I went to the swimming pool. I swam lengths, I counted the laps.

Sandra and Kim didn't swim.

Kim oversaw housekeeping. She was married to Doep. She kept to herself.

Sandra lived with Lloyd, the lodge manager. She managed the female staff. Sandra gave me a silk scarf from the curio shop. She let me choose the khaki uniform that suited me best. She let me watch taped episodes of *Thirty Something* on her TV when Lloyd was away. I was addicted to *Thirty Something*. I was almost thirty, I was almost married. I was watching my life as it might be if we left the lodge and returned to the city.

If we left the lodge.

I felt worse after my mother phoned.

I was on the reception desk when she called. My mother was excited. She told me about the state president's speech. He had unbanned all the political organisations. He had freed all the political prisoners.

I was not invited to watch Lloyd and Sandra's TV the day Nelson Mandela was released. Doep and Burt went. I passed Doep on the pathway after lunch. I couldn't help myself, I had to ask: 'What does he look like?'

'They're still waiting for him,' Doep said. He used another word for 'they'. 'There are thousands of them and a few traitors like you.'

Mandela was free but nothing changed at the game lodge. Nothing except Rexford was fired. Lloyd fired him for wearing an African National Congress T-shirt in the workers' compound.

Rexford was one of the trackers. One of the voteless men from a nearby village who knew the land better than any of the rangers. Trackers sat above the Land Rover's left wheel and kept their eyes peeled. Ndlopfu, they would say, when they spotted signs of elephant. Nghala, when they saw lion tracks. The trackers spoke Xitsonga so as not to give tourists false hope. The rangers would radio the other Land Rovers. If the tracks led to a kill, all the Land Rovers converged like hyenas.

I arrived at the lodge with a ring. A thin gold band with blue specks. We chose it before my final exams. The sapphires kept distracting me as I wrote.

None of the lodge staff seemed excited about our engagement. Doep and Kim were the only married couple. Sandra said Lloyd would never marry again. Allan was married but his wife and child had gone back to the city.

I felt worse in the autumn.

It was too cold to swim. I was not allowed to leave camp

on my own. There was nowhere to walk inside the camp. The swept pathways that linked reception with the dining room and chalets were short. The paths that led to the staff houses and workers' compound were close by, hidden behind screens of bamboo.

I walked past the workshop to the entrance of the compound but I didn't go inside. I had no friends inside. The young woman who cleaned reception and the curio shop could say hello and goodbye in English. I could say hello and how are you in Xitsonga. I chatted to the kitchen staff but it was just small talk. I wanted to see the babies in the compound but I didn't want to see the matchbox houses with their zinc roofs or the separate ablution block. I was not doing research. I was not there to ask questions.

The staff accommodation was for the white employees. There was a long block of single rooms with their own bathrooms, a thatched house for Lloyd and Sandra, a thatched cottage for Doep and Kim, a few thatched rondavels for couples.

We tried to make our rondavel home. We had our bed from the city with its Indian bedspread and a bookcase with my novels and your reference books. We had a tape deck, cassettes by Abdullah Ibrahim and Hugh Masekela and a shortwave radio with scratchy reception.

We had separate schedules. You left before dawn for the morning game drive while I was sleeping. You ate your meals with the guests, I ate with the female staff. When you had time off I was working in the curio shop. When I left the boma bonfire at night you were still drinking with the tourists.

The staff gave us a party before we left for our wedding. Kim gave me advice: 'Always put your man first.' Sandra gave me a carved wooden bowl from the curio shop.

Doep and Burt gave you an iron girder. They chained it to your ankle. Doep held up the key for everyone to see and threw it away into the bush. You had to carry the girder wherever you went that night. You had to drink every pint of beer laced with peppermint liqueur they placed in front of you.

I placed a chair next to your side of our bed for the girder. I placed a bucket close to your head and emptied your vomit throughout the night. You carried the girder to the workshop at dawn. You were about to use an angle grinder to cut the chain when Doep appeared and threw the spare key at your feet.

I felt worse after we returned from our wedding at the sea, our sunlit honeymoon.

I felt worse in the winter.

The rondavel was dark, our bedspread and books were covered with bits of old thatch.

I felt worse in the air-conditioned curio shop.

The door stayed shut. I was not allowed to read. I had to look alert. I had to check the stock each week. Gold chains went missing. I told Sandra and she said, 'Thank you for telling me.' I wrote down my purchases. My purchases of chocolate bars. I ate more each day.

I received post. I received letters from my mother, from your mother.

I received my university honours degree, cum laude.

I received a seminar paper about the genesis of the national park. It wasn't created to conserve lions and leopards. Predators were considered vermin until they proved to be the park's main attraction. The national park was established to heal the rift between white people. To unite Afrikaans and English speakers around a sentimental affection for the natural landscape. And a tightly controlled park would prevent black communities from using the land for subsistence hunting and foraging.

I wrote letters to our wedding guests thanking them for their gifts, the pile of presents still in their boxes in your parents' house. I wrote: *We look forward to using the lovely milk jug/ silver-plated cake knife/set of glasses once we leave the game lodge and set up home.*

❖

Sometimes you speak about the way lions warm up their vocal cords. The way they stretch their mouths wide, almost gagging, the way the roar starts low and husky at the back of their throats, then the sound gets louder and louder each time. You speak about the leopards you saw. Your three yingwe sightings. The last one in a tree right outside the camp fence. You took me to see it.

Sometimes I think about the scops owl that lived in the tree on the way to the kitchen. Whenever I hear a Diederik's cuckoo I remember the stunned fledgling I found near reception. I cupped it in my hands for a few minutes while its heart raced, before it flew away. I looked it up in your bird book. I checked its colouring, confirmed its call: *deed-deed-deed-deed-er-ick*.

We arrive in the winter

We arrive in the winter. We arrive too soon, too soon for me. My nose and eyes are streaming. I want to be here rather than the place we were before, but I would rather be in the place we were before that.

I sit on a bench and look at the wind-chopped lagoon. I look across the water at fynbos hills scarred by pine trees. The sun is weak. The taaibos beside me is covered with caterpillars, hairy yellow and black caterpillars that leave spikes in your thumb if you touch them. They are eating every leaf.

'Come,' you say. You lead me inside. You make me stand at one end of the dinner table, you stand at the other. You draw lines with burnt cork on the yellowwood. 'These are your goals, these are mine,' you say. You demonstrate how to flick a beer-cap across the table with your thumb and forefinger. You score a goal first time.

On weekdays you put on overalls and leave the house.

Our friends arrive in the summer. Jen and Matthew and Patty and the rest of the gang. They stay for weeks. They sleep anywhere, everywhere. It doesn't matter because no one sleeps. We talk, we laugh, we drink, we play cards. We play volleyball on the strip of lawn between the house and the lagoon. We fry eggs and bacon, slice bread and cheese, braai meat. We sit around, we talk, we laugh, we drink. We sing. We smoke cigarettes. We smoke grass.

We take off our clothes and run into the lagoon. The stars are bright, the tide is out, the water is knee high. The neighbours' lights are on, there are fishing boats in the channel. We don't care, we keep walking. We cut our feet on horse mussels and feel no pain. We sink into sandy indentations covered with sea grass, we wallow in the cool salty water, we lie flat to soak our hair.

Jen walks out of the lagoon with water streaming down her back, down the planes of her face. Jen the poker queen who never cries. She can't stop, she keeps apologising.

We talk to our friends, you and I, we don't talk to each other. We fall into bed drunk and exhausted. In the morning you wrap a kikoi around your waist and rush downstairs to join the early risers.

I want to spend the day in bed reading.

I want to make a cake. 'Then you must make one,' Jen says. We eat it warm.

Matthew wants to eat a burger. We drive into town. We eat burgers or pizzas with stringy yellow cheese or pasta with cream and ham. We share a salad of sliced lettuce and pale tomatoes. We drink cheap wine and strong beer. We split the bill. Some of us have jobs, some of us are interns, some of us are still studying. One of us arrived here too soon and has no prospect of work.

Jen wants to go to a karaoke bar. Jen and Patty know every word of *Biko*. They know every word of *Jerusalem*. I know every word of *So Long Marianne*. None of these songs are on the list but we go up on stage. 'This one,' Jen decides. *All the leaves are brown and the sky is grey.*

Rosalind

Rosalind woke up as the afternoon sun left the deck. She looked around. Everyone had paired off. The forest beyond the lawn had blurred into corrugations of green and black, beckoning her like fingers. She lowered herself off the cottage deck and moved through the long grass. Perhaps a walk would make her feel better.

But the stream was the colour of sewage. Forest ferns kept their new fronds tightly coiled as if withholding pleasure. Stepping stones wobbled threateningly underfoot as she leapt across the freezing water.

A footpath sucked her into the forest. Garish mushrooms and fungi burst out of fallen trees like radioactive cancers. A single bird called, sounding panicky. The overlapping canopy blocked out most of the remaining light. Twigs snapped with an ominous crack. Rustling leaves and falling branches startled her. Every step released a stench of loamy decay.

Just as she decided to turn back, the mist fell. If she stretched out her arm she could barely see her hand. She turned back anyway. Or had she turned back already? Was she walking deeper into the forest? Rosalind spun around and stumbled on, panic rising, tears forming. Spiderwebs snapped across her face. Low slung branches and thorny barks bashed and scratched her as she scrambled over lichen-covered trunks that had fallen across the path.

She quickened her pace. The path rose steeply. Maybe

there'd be no mist at the top of the hill and she would have a clear view of the cottage and the way back. They must have lit the lamps by now. She broke into a jog, gulping for breath. The mist had soaked up the heat of the day and she ran faster to warm up. Just as she was sure she'd reached the top of the hill the ground fell away and she bounced down the cliff like a boulder, glancing off trees and rocks as she picked up pace.

Rosalind woke on a bed of forest ferns. Her face felt wet and sticky, she licked her lips and tasted blood. She spoke to her arms and legs but they wouldn't respond.

She gazed up at branches and leaves sprinkled with sparkling stars. She could feel the forest breathing out, releasing an avalanche of oxygen, all for her. She breathed in deeply and out slowly, as all pain and tension seeped from her fingers and toes.

Rosalind raised her head and saw that her hands and feet were covered in lichen. Long creepers snaking down from the trees encircled her arms and legs. A handful of leaves silvered by starlight floated down to her stomach. She laid her head back down feeling her long loose hair take root in the soil. She closed her eyes.

A garden full

Hot pink sky when we left the beach. When I was two. Dad had the umbrella. Ma had me. Kai had his bucket and truck. That's what Ma says. Dad too when he visits.

We walked up the beach. Up the dune. Up the path. Past the restaurant. Along the road. Lots of people walked too, Ma says. Dogs and people going to the beach. Kids and people coming off the beach. I was too tired to walk, Ma says. Old people with sticks. Running people with dogs. Hello they said. Hello we said. Tall man says Hello little boy. Say hello, Kai, Ma says. Hello says Kai.

Along the road. Up our street. Our house. Grass, tree, doors, windows, beds, shower. It's what we needed, Ma says. It was a busy year. Time for holiday.

Hot and hungry in the house. Sausage for Kai. Milk for me. Dad sweaty. Ma sits against the window, holds me drinking bottle. Kai says run outside please-please-please. Okay says Dad but you're showering after me. Okay but just for a little while says Ma.

Kai runs through the house out the back door round the house in the front door. Out round through. Out round through. Me drinking. Ma resting. Dad washing. Kai out round through. Out round through. Light going. Beetles buzzing. Dad clean. Bottle empty. Ma calling. Dad calling. Ma shouting. Dad running. Me crying.

If only I'd showered later, Dad says.

If only I'd turned and looked out the window, Ma says.

Tall man lifts Kai into tree. Kai galloping fast horse yee haw, riding big bike vroom vroom, climbing high ladder up up.

Tall man says: Kai you like trees? Come with me I have a garden full.

❖

The body of male child.

Height: 1.28m.

Estimated Mass: 25kg.

A ligature abrasion mark lies in the neck posteriorly.

Abrasions in the neck anteriorly.

Cause of death was: Consistent with strangulation and the consequences thereof.

The body was clothed in: A brown top with the word 'Club'. A pair of brown shorts.

Jay & the lynx

Jay visited an Oudtshoorn wildlife ranch and spoke to the owner. He wanted a lynx. Not all men would be suited to keeping a lynx, but Jay was tall with strong shoulders. He had thick eyebrows and size twelve feet.

Jay had twenty-twenty vision. Once in the Karoo he saw a leopard. We were having sundowners in a Gamkaberg camp when we heard a snort of alarm. Jay stared at the cliff. 'Klipspringer,' he said. I got up to fetch the binoculars. By the time I returned it was too late. The buck was gone. Jay said it had moved so fast it seemed to be flying, or falling. The pursuing animal was almost vertical. 'Baboon,' I guessed. But Jay shook his head. Its tail had been the length of its body: a leopard.

The leopard was Jay's favourite animal but he knew he couldn't keep one as a pet. That's where the lynx came in. A lynx would be almost as good. A lynx would be a more manageable size, as big as some dogs. A month later the wildlife ranch rang. A caracal cub was available. A few hundred rand for five kilograms of tawny fur with black tufty ears, eyes outlined with kohl and sharp white teeth.

Like the lynx, Jay was solitary. He was a loner. He spent hours out fishing on the Knysna lagoon. He waited until the grunters were tailing in a shallow spot, then he grabbed his little yellow boat and rowed off. He returned with supper and an empty beer bottle. It was always a bottle, never a can because it wasn't as easy to piss into a can.

One night he hooked a large stingray. He was drinking a bottle of Calitzdorp Port that time, floating near Land's End, when the ray took his bait. At first he thought he had hooked a kob, but there was a strange splash, an upwelling of water. A few minutes later he realised the boat was being pulled out towards the open sea in slow steady loops. Jay looked down. He saw the edge of the stingray's wing-flaps outlined in phosphorescence as it swam underneath him. It was as wide as the boat. The ray worked its way free at the Heads. Jay returned home wide-eyed. The next day he used a jigsaw to cut a piece of hardboard into the shape of a stingray. He painted a miniature fisherman in a rowing boat on the edge of its body.

Jay was an artist. Soon after we got together he made a mobile with tiny tilapia he'd found on the banks of Hartbeespoort Dam. He dried them and sprayed them with silver paint. He didn't ask if I liked the mobile. He arrived at the newspaper and hung it above my desk. The vegetarian sub-editor wrinkled her nose. After a few summer thunderstorms the fish swelled. When they started to stink I took the mobile down. I wrapped it in a plastic bag and stowed it in my desk drawer.

Jay didn't go out fishing the night after the wildlife ranch phoned. We sat on the deck. The moon was bright. The lagoon lapped like bathwater. Jay was happy. He spoke quietly about how he would take the lynx for walks around Leisure Isle at night when the tide was low. It would follow him everywhere and sleep on the kitchen porch or under the taaibos near the rowing boat. It had been born in captivity so was accustomed to humans. He would give it a bottle and raw meat as it grew older. He made it sound a bit like a dog. But lynx were different, Jay said. Their droppings were segmented and turned white in the sun. They were opportunistic hunters. They ate domestic cats.

I stared at Jay. We had a cat called Sugar. I got him in Johannesburg. Jay's cousin phoned me one day and said she had found a stray tabby kitten with a squirrel tail. Sugar hid under my bed for days but grew into the friendliest cat. When I moved to Knysna I brought him with me. He never liked living on Leisure Isle half as much as Yeoville. The lagoon startled him and the coastal sun burnt cancerous growths into his pink nose and white face.

Jay and Sugar never really hit it off. Jay liked kissing cats. He said their fur smelt like musk and wild sage. He would get down on all fours and fight with them. He'd let them catch onto his arm and drag them across the floor or shake them playfully until they sank their claws into his flesh. He was always surprised when he saw the blood. His favourite sparring partner was our friend's cat Yagar who scratched his face more than once. Sugar didn't meet these needs. He didn't like rough games, and Jay said he was too fluffy to kiss.

After Jay cancelled his order for the caracal cub, he avoided our cat. As if Sugar was somehow to blame for being lynx food. He spent more time alone on the lagoon. He rowed back long after I had fallen asleep.

A few weeks later Jay arrived home smiling. He was holding a furry ball. He called him Blaasop, though he looked nothing like a puffer fish to me. Jay pointed out the stripes, spots and russet tint to the backs of the ears typical of the African wild cat. As soon as the kitten had grown a bit, Jay dipped Blaasop's feet into the lagoon at low tide to get him used to salt water. They'd go for walks at night and Blaasop would return with wet legs and burrs matted into his coat.

Sugar took to Blaasop from the start, they groomed each other and sat on twin gateposts as regal as any lions. But Sugar never joined in when Blaasop wrestled with Jay. He would wait on the upturned boat when they disappeared on their nightly strolls.

Sugar was sitting on the boat one afternoon when two Jack Russells attacked him. Jay and Blaasop arrived too late to intervene. Jay never forgot the look of terror on the cat's face. Blaasop was next. Jay couldn't speak after he found him under a milkwood tree, perfectly intact except for a hole bored into his belly. The evidence pointed to a genet.

Jay vowed no more cats. We moved to the other side of the estuary, further away from the ocean and closer to the river. The vow didn't last. Our next two tabbies, both from Animal Welfare, died in quick succession: Jessie got fat and died on our bed. Crunchie was hit by a car.

I reminded Jay, no more cats but he went back to Animal Welfare and returned with Doolie, the offspring of a pedigree Siamese mother and a roving tom, a silky silver tabby, a beauty with an ugly voice. As a kitten Doolie leapt out of an upstairs window to chase a bird and landed easily. He stalked a hadeda five times his size. Being neutered only seemed to increase his hunting lust. He ate everything he could find, bells around the neck were no deterrent. Doolie caught grasshoppers, lizards, striped mice, shrews, dormice and rats. He brought the rats inside. He carried pigeons into the lounge and tormented them until the carpet was strewn with feathers. He killed and ate robins, drongos, doves and sunbirds. Jay tied a dead sunbird around Doolie's neck to no effect. He prised open the cat's jaws and freed an olive thrush, waxbills, weavers and canaries. When Doolie killed a buff-spotted flufftail Jay threw the cat into the frog pond. But Doolie had no concept of cause and effect. We bought more bells.

Doolie made us do strange things. Jay went on an animal communication course. He learnt that you couldn't use words to tell animals what to do. You had to send them images. Everyone had to bring a photograph of a problem pet to the course, look deep into its pixilated eyes and send it pictures. Jay tried to send Doolie an image of himself in the garden. In the image Jay was standing very still, his head, shoulders and outstretched arms were covered with sunbirds.

Deep down Jay believed Doolie was karma. Doolie had been sent to teach him a lesson. To punish Jay for all the white-eyes, doves and rock pigeons he had shot with pellet guns. All the guinea fowl he had killed with shotguns. Jay started releasing the fish he caught. He stopped fishing.

Doolie's appetite for killing, however, only increased. He often disappeared for whole nights on hunting expeditions. We had become accustomed to these absences but when he didn't return after two days we became concerned. We looked in cupboards. We made *Have you seen our cat* signs. We walked all the cat paths we knew, crawled under bushes, interrogated our neighbours. Jay sent Doolie images. We phoned vets and Animal Welfare.

I emailed a cat psychic who asked for a photograph of Doolie and a bank deposit. She told me Doolie was fine. He was having fun with a black cat. He had just caught a mouse and was going to have a nap. He wasn't ready to come home yet. I wrote back and said, *Tell him we miss him. Tell him I'll open a tin of tuna when he returns.*

Next she wrote that Doolie wanted to come home but he was injured. He was staying in a tiny house with people who gave him love. He was sleeping in the arms of a young girl. Jay was watching the news one night when, behind the man being interviewed, he saw a little girl holding a silver tabby. Jay said the cat looked right at him.

We kept going over and over our last night with Doolie. Jay said it was while he was brushing his teeth that he heard a strangled screech. He went out onto the upstairs deck and looked out over the dark garden. But all he could hear were the frogs.

People came to us with their stories and theories. We lived three streets below a tree-covered hill that stretched to the sea and bordered on a nature reserve. Our neighbours listed the cats that had vanished in our suburb that year. There were seven or more, here one day then not. Some blamed owls, others eagles, but Jay knew who the predator was. Walking in the fynbos bordering the plantation he had stopped to pick up a discarded beer bottle. That's when he saw the white segmented droppings matted with silver-grey fur.

Contractions

Ripple lost her baby in a dream. A dream so real she told no one. She felt complicit. Her mind was full of *Damage*. She watched the film twice, watched the actors coupling on the floor, watched the young star want the father and the son.

Rip wanted to read the novel, but could only find the author's second book, *Sin*. She read it while the nurse took her temperature. Her uterus was irritable; the baby's heart a galloping horse on the monitor. Rip read to calm herself. The nurse took the book out of her hands and shook her head. Books like that weren't good for baby. She called Rip mommy although she was only seven months pregnant.

A few nights later Rip had the dream. She dreamt she was in the labour ward, breathing through her contractions, when a doctor – with the nice face of the GP scheduled to deliver her baby – said labour wasn't progressing normally and she would need an emergency Caesar. In the dream Rip woke up from the anaesthetic with an empty bassinet beside her bed; a nurse said her baby was stillborn.

Two months after the nightmare, Rip was in the labour ward of the Provincial Hospital, her feet in stirrups. The nice-looking GP was pulling on latex gloves and preparing to examine her. Rip had brought her radio into the labour room. President Nelson Mandela was delivering his first state of the nation address. He was speaking slowly and seriously, pausing to let each phrase sink in as he quoted Ingrid Jonker: *The child* ...

is not dead … the child … lifts his fists … The GP told Rip to breathe during his examination.

Jay walked up and down the labour room. He hated waiting. He hated hospitals. The big city hospital had been the worst. Those smirking, judgemental nurses. There was always the implication that Jay was having all the fun. All he had to do was jerk off. Rip had to have hormone injections to release multiple ova and quadruple PMS symptoms. She needed an anaesthetic so her clutch of eggs could be harvested, mixed with Jay's sperm, and inserted into one of her fallopian tubes. Rip would experience minor discomfort after the procedure, the fertility specialists said. They never spoke about the discomfort of having to ejaculate in a neon-lit cubicle while the laboratory staff waited for Jay's jar of sperm. The cubicle was decorated with a poster of a teenage couple about to kiss while the sun set between them. There was a chaste pile of women's magazines in the corner. Jay looked out the window, focused on a petrol station's logo – a leering rabbit – and fulfilled his obligations.

Rip menstruated two and a half weeks after the procedure. She cried, like she did every month. There was nothing wrong with her, the specialists said. It was Jay. His sperm. Mobility was okay but motility was shot. His swimmers were deformed. Jay blamed the fucker who kicked him in the balls all those years ago. All around them people were breeding like rabbits – even friends with their quota of offspring were having mistakes – while every single month Rip's period underscored his failure.

After the fertility procedure failed Jay's mother began knitting a striped blanket. She started with grey, then switched to yellow, pink and blue. It was hideous, Jay's father said. He said that about everything she knitted. He would rather she spent all her time typing his manuscripts. Every row she knitted was further proof that he had written nothing new, his creative juices had dried up. Jay's mother clicked away with her needles. She told Jay that by the time the blanket was finished Rip would be pregnant.

Jay's mother never spoke about the time Rip phoned and asked to meet during her lunch break. They sat in a car and Rip cried about not falling pregnant. Rip was unhinged, of course. Jay's mother could hardly believe what she was asking: if Jay's sperm was no good perhaps his father could make a donation? Men far older had fathered children. Jay's mother patted Rip's hand and passed her a tissue. She said she knew Rip and Jay would have a baby. She had seen the child in a dream. All they needed to do was go on holiday.

It was after the holiday that Rip fell pregnant. A couple of months afterwards. She glowed and swelled and carried on cycling to work until the end of her second trimester. She walked every day and did antenatal exercises. She read books about what-to-expect-when-you're-expecting and chapters about when-things-go-wrong. Nothing went wrong until her uterus turned irritable, so just to be safe Rip stopped working. It had been a temporary job anyway. She voted with the special voters in an old age home one day before the rest of the country queued for the first democratic elections.

Jay came back from voting with shining eyes. He spoke about the jubilant first-time voters but he refused to discuss baby names. He called their fetus Grisbelda. Other men in the antenatal classes spoke as if they shared their wives' wombs. Jay didn't want to count any chickens or jinx anything. He thought about the men who had visited his house in the last year. The plumber who rebuilt the septic tank about nine months ago. The dark-haired plumber.

In the labour room Rip was breathing and trying to concentrate on Mandela's voice *The child is not dead ... not at Langa ... nor at Nyanga ...* The GP pressed against her cervix. It hurt but the pain was bearable. *Nor at Orlando ... nor at Sharpeville ...*

A nurse switched on the monitor and the baby's galloping horse heart drowned out the radio. The doctor withdrew his hand and looked at Rip. Speaking slowly and calmly he said her cervix wasn't dilating. The pressure on the baby's skull was putting too much strain on its brain. He advised that the baby be delivered by emergency Caesar immediately.

Jay was standing outside the hospital theatre when a nurse emerged with a bundle with very little hair, none of it black.

Rip woke up from her general anaesthetic with a drip in her arm. The curtains around her hospital bed were drawn. She turned her head and saw the empty plastic bassinet. The curtains parted and a nurse appeared with a bundle in a striped knitted blanket. A bundle with eyes that looked straight at Rip, with a mouth that clamped around her nipple.

Nothing else mattered. Everything else was peripheral: Jay, his parents, doctors, nurses, friends, flowers, fruit, radio news reports, newspapers with headlines about reconciliation, magazines screaming about genocide *There are no devils left in hell*.

Confessions

I didn't know if I had enough love. I loved your brother so much. I had loved him for three years. You were sleepy when you were delivered. They should have left you in me longer before the Caesar. They should have let you decide when you wanted to be born. You wouldn't look at me when the doctor handed you to me, they gave you to me for just a minute before the nurse took you away. They said you were cold. You needed to be in the incubator. Your grandmother saw my face. She made them bring you back. You didn't look at me, you were sleeping. But you woke up when your brother arrived. You turned to look at him, you had heard his voice for months. You drank from me sleepily. You were content, peaceful. You slept in my arms.

Your grandparents said your brother was standing on a chair looking out the window when your dad phoned from the hospital with the news. They came upstairs and told him he had a brother. They said he whooped and ran round and round his room.

I felt guilty when I brought you home. I was sitting in your brother's room nursing you when he came and asked for milk. It gushed into his mouth and he stepped away, betrayed. The look in his eyes. Am I no longer enough? Are you no longer mine?

On your first night home, I lay between you and your brother. I had my arms around both of you. I looked at your sleeping brother, his such-loved faced, his cheeks still mottled with emotion. I turned and looked at you, I couldn't look away.

❖

It was me. We were late. It was your brother's first sports tour. He was young. He would be gone for a week. He didn't have the correct clothes. The cool clothes. I bought him long shorts and a vest. Too big as usual. Because he would grow. We left in a whirl. In a rush. I heard something as we reversed out the driveway. I said 'What was that?' You both said 'What was what?' I kept driving. I kept checking that your brother had his sandwich for the trip, his wallet. The bus was waiting. We were late. We weren't the last to arrive. The bus left and we drove home, you and I. The house was quiet without your brother. I worried about his trip, whether the bus was safe, whether the older boys were kind. I felt uneasy. Your friend came to play. I drank tea with his mother. I put a chicken in the oven to roast. I filled the cats' bowls. I made a salad. Your father came home at six. He saw Jessie eating her pellets. He said 'Where's Crunchie?' I knew then. I knew before he found your cat near the neighbour's fence. She was lying on her side. Stiff. Your father put her in a box. He took her to the vet the next day. The vet said her ribs were crushed. Your father asked did we hear anything? Did we hear a car slam on brakes perhaps? Anything at all? I said we heard nothing. I said nothing.

Stone cold

A churchyard in the middle of town. Two stone churches, a church hall, graves, trees, flowers, paths. A body under a pine tree.

A low stone wall surrounds the churchyard. Two layers of hand-picked, hand-placed stones. Each stone is different. Some are pointy, others concave, like seats. A man sits on a stone seat: a young man of twenty-two with braids. A young woman stands next to him: a girl of eighteen with long light-brown hair. They talk. They smoke.

A gibbous moon. A few hours past midnight. A truck driver delivering bread. The driver sees a man sitting on the stone wall under a street light talking to a girl. He sees his braids. He sees the girl's long hair, her jeans and black crop top that shows her stomach. He drives around the block, sees them again. He watches them until the robots turn green.

A fisherman walks up from the lagoon at first light, walks through town, takes a short cut through the churchyard. He sees a body. He sees a pair of jeans, he places them over the body, over the face. I wanted to cover her, he says.

A mother rolls up the cord of her vacuum cleaner. A phone rings. The mother speaks into the receiver. She says: It can't be. I'm meeting her for coffee this morning.

Two night clubs on opposite corners of Main Street: Zanzibar and Stones. The young cross the road between them, looking for the better music, the better crowd.

A Main Street flat in a building alongside a churchyard: a long-haired girl's flat. A young man with dark eyes: the long-haired girl's flatmate. They are hotel interns together – friends, then lovers, then friends. The long-haired girl is jealous when he kisses her friend. She forbids him to. The flatmate puts a note on her pillow. It reads: *Fuck off and die.*

A forensic scientist says she has only seen so much blood and flesh beneath a victim's fingernails once before.

A flatmate comes home from Zanzibar with a girl on each arm. He makes coffee. A long-haired girl comes home too. She asks for tea. Her flatmate leaves the tea-bag in. He takes the coffee and the girls into his room. He shuts the door.

A disc jockey with a roll of fat peeping through his braids. A roll of fat where the back of his skull meets his neck. A disc jockey from Stones. He watches the long-haired girl dance, dances with her, tells her she always skips a beat.

A policeman tells a mother: I can promise you your daughter fought.

A young woman with an elfin face: the mother of the disc jockey's little sons (but not the mother of his little daughter). She sees the long deep scratches down his back. She says: What are these fuck-marks?

A powerfully built father of four sons, a retired prison chief, with a roll of fat behind his neck. A mother with a closed face, a cancer survivor. They are in the courtroom every day, in the bench behind the dock, wearing white – for innocence – on judgment day.

A mother who will never be happy again, who keeps all her daughter's things, who inhales the scent of her unwashed clothes, wears her jewellery. A silent father who works in a factory fixing machines, who wants to fix someone.

A disc jockey says he and a long-haired girl went to a parking area to have sex. He describes the positions, how they stood and sat, how she enjoyed it. He tells the judge about his favourite gig pants, tight-fitting corduroys which display his features nicely. He says all the girls want to sleep with him.

Messages on two cell phones. Short joking messages between a long-haired girl and a friend. Messages sent back and forth. Messages sent at the same time that the disc jockey claims he and the long-haired girl were having sex.

A post-mortem report:

> *Soil on the face, in the mouth, pharynx and upper*
> *trachea.*
> *Scattered abrasions of the body.*
> *Cause of death: Asphyxia due to aspiration of soil.*
> *Mechanism of Death: Asphyxia.*
> *Manner of Death: Homicide.*

Too many footprints in the churchyard. The police don't find the footprints that matter. Too many cigarette butts around the stone wall and in the churchyard. The police don't collect the ones that matter.

Blood and tissue recovered from a long-haired girl's fingernails. The long fingernails with tips she painted white. There is a

DNA match for the tissue. Semen found inside her and on her underwear. There is a DNA match for the semen.

A flatmate says goodbye to two girls in the early hours of morning. He sees the tea-bag floating in the cold tea. He sees the long-haired girl's keys on the table. He sends her an SMS saying he's leaving the door unlocked. He goes to sleep.

A judge says the victim died literally eating soil.

A man with a gun. A muscled man who likes to tell pretty girls to call him if they are in trouble. He switches off his phone one night. He misses a call from a long-haired girl.

A judge says the accused shows no remorse and at times seems proud of what had happened. He says he should spend the rest of his natural life behind bars.

A model prisoner with a roll of fat behind his neck is studying to be a teacher. He is helping other inmates to complete their schooling. He is hoping to be released early for good behaviour.

A body under a pine tree in a churchyard. A young woman's body dressed in a black long-sleeved cropped jersey, black underwear, one green sock, bangles and a silver bracelet. She is lying on her back. Her long light-brown hair is fanned out above her on the ground. Her arms are raised. She is scratched and smeared with dirt and blood. She has been dragged from a place where the ground is scuffed. A place closer to a small block of flats. Closer to a low stone wall.

Swimming with crocodiles

I wear the backless dress I wore to my sister's wedding, a blue cotton dress with a high neck. I wade a long way through shallow tropical water and breaking waves to reach the ship. My child walks next to me, his head as high as my waist. I wear the backless dress back to front.

Someone has been staying in my cabin, the bed is rumpled. I am looking for a yoga room, we go from place to place searching.

I watch a video of myself in the back to front dress. My nipples are sprouting soft black strands of cotton. My son and I are silent, comfortable together. I watch the video calmly.

I notice tufts of long grass rooted in my side. We find the perfect room, it is unfurnished, with a wooden floor and only three walls. We are swimming with crocodiles. I tug at the grassy tufts in my side, they come away easily. The room opens on to a sand dune which slopes down to the sea. The crocodiles come up for breath, they are just men in reptile suits.

I find a nylon thread above my hip. Sand lies heaped on the floorboards. The island children come to talk to us. I pull on the thread, it comes out and out.

My son finds a treasure on the dune: a drinking glass. I offer the island children a banana. I pull and pull the thread above my hip, there is no end. I take the glass to wash it but press too hard, it breaks into three pieces. The children shake their heads, they have all the bananas they can eat. I use both hands to yank the thread and deliver a trawling net.

5

Skin

I hear about your skeleton while I am making muffins. I switch off the whirring hand-mixer, press the phone to my ear: Your skeleton, found in the Knysna forest.

I think you must be one of the women who vanished in these dense yellowwood forests which hide elephants, which swallowed a crashed helicopter for seven years. Maybe you are Seteline, the missing teenage schoolgirl. Or Rosalind, the drama student who disappeared in the sixties. I see my by-line on the newspaper's front page.

I listen some more. You are male. Your skeleton was found in a plantation of evenly spaced pine trees beside the national road.

I put the muffins in the oven. Set the timer. Check whether my son needs help with his homework. Sit down at my desk and make two calls.

The police have opened an inquest docket into your death but suspect no foul play. The plantation manager gives me your name, Karl, your age, thirty. He says his men were cutting saplings when they found you. I email five paragraphs to a Cape Town newspaper. I collect my older son from hockey.

Late at night, I look out at the dark trees in the garden. I can see you. Your flesh consumed by animals and insects, your bones bleached by the elements, scattered by the wind and birds of prey. I can see the porcelain veneer on your teeth, your black leather jacket with all its zips – your identity book in one pocket, a Nokia phone in another, an MP3 player in a third.

Through medical friends I learn more. You had been missing for a year. You were a patient at the Tranquillity drug rehabilitation clinic outside town.

I drive northwest up a long tarred road and along a sandy track. Tranquillity is a motley collection of buildings on the edge of a plantation. I sit on a brown couch in reception and wait for Mark, your psychologist. I watch six residents on the stoep outside. They seem to be shifting felled Christmas trees from one pile to another.

I spend two hours on that couch. I listen to Mark, his quiet voice. I change tapes twice. Mark consults a cardboard folder on his lap. Two recovering addicts-turned-counsellors, Jeffrey and Paul, join us at the end. They stand beside Mark and share a few memories. They talk slowly, pausing between sentences.

I drive home with a bursting head, collect my sons from friends, hear them arguing over whose turn it is on the computer. I pour brandy over the Christmas cake, wrap presents. I plan the Christmas dinner I'll cook for my family and in-laws – seafood curry just to be different.

I walk on the beach alone and think of you. What I know about you. Fragments inside a thin cardboard file. Mark says you never told your story. You gave him the bare minimum, the bones.

Junior school: parents divorce; Attention Deficit Disorder diagnosis; Ritalin.

High school: cannabis daily; experiments with LSD and mandrax; arrest for mandrax possession; two months in jail awaiting trial; suspended sentence; two months in a state psychiatric and drug rehabilitation centre; matriculates.

After school: abandons hotel management studies; works as a waiter; drinks heavily; starts using heroin at twenty-five.

I swim in the sea. I watch my sons surf. After each wave I wait for their heads to resurface. I think about you. I think about me, my sheltered childhood, my sheltering mothering. I know

101

something about isolation. I know something about drinking before I can dance, how weed makes colours glow, how cocaine makes words barrel out of my mouth.

I want to speak to your mother. Your mother the nursing sister who lives in another city. She says she will talk face to face but keeps postponing our meeting. She stops taking my calls. I want to ask about you as a baby, as a young boy.

Mark says you were more in tune with your father. Your much older father who died alone on his farm when you were a teenager.

Mark says your mother was anxious for you, she made you feel anxious. He says she did her best. She set boundaries but allowed you to make your own choices. She cared for you. She took out a bank loan to pay for your expensive dental work. She paid for your rehab – the first stint of eight months, the second of two and a half years. She bought the appliances you needed. She got you to thirty.

You make me anxious for my sons. Mark speaks about parents who are inconsistent, who over-indulge their children, set no boundaries, shield them from the consequences of their choices. I see myself driving back to the school with the lunch boxes my sons left behind, with the sports gear they forgot to pack, topping up their allowances.

I go to the gym. I cover murder trials and local government elections. I report on the rising rate of HIV infections. I buy food and cook. I make rye sandwiches for lunch. I make chocolate cake for birthdays, I use my mother's recipe.

I want to speak to your wife Jolene, but she lives far away. She might still be in prison. Mark says you introduced her to heroin. I pull wet clothes out of the washing machine, hang them on racks in the sun. I know which colours you both wore on your wedding day. I conjure up a hazy image, you all in black, thin body, sharp cheekbones, long dark hair in your eyes; Jolene in a long red dress. I can't see her face. I imagine a fragile Goth princess.

At Tranquillity letters home are compulsory. You sent Jolene short faxes. You called her Jinxie, used Afrikaans diminutives: her little arms, her little voice. You said sorry.

I pack the dishwasher, switch it on. I want to speak to India, your girlfriend at Tranquillity, the last person to see you alive. Mark says she died in a city rehab.

India. Jeffrey blames her for your death. He says you messed with the wrong woman at the wrong time. Mark says relationships between rehab residents are discouraged. Being in love gives a false euphoria, stops people from dealing with the issues that led to their addiction.

I open a tin for our tabby. I see you opening tins of tomatoes in the Tranquillity kitchen, chopping endless carrots. I see you stuck in the mind-numbing routine of construction work, carrying planks, hammering nails. The grinding noise of power tools. Your frustration when they won't do what you want. Your surprise when a jigsaw slices off the tip of your finger.

I see you as Mark described you at Tranquillity's compulsory church services: silent, huddled into your black hoodie, just the tips of your fingers sticking out. I imagine the magic India brings to your dull repetitive days. India, the seasoned heroin junkie, the talented special effects make-up artist, the rehab veteran. I imagine a take no shit beauty. Dazzling defiance. The two of you against the world.

I answer emails for my husband's business. I draw up spreadsheets for company expenses. Our cat walks across the keyboard. I remember Paul said you tamed the wild cats at Tranquillity. I see you putting out saucers of water and kibbles, sitting very still nearby, moving closer to the saucers every day until the cats rub themselves against your knees and elbows, your back, until the black cat lets you stroke her. I see you bringing scraps of meat from the kitchen for the black cat, after she gives birth in your drawer, playing with her kittens as they grow. Your sadness after you deposit them at Animal Welfare.

Our tabby curls up on a pile of invoices. I remember Mark talking about the time he brought you back to Tranquillity for the second time, after your mother phoned him. He fetched you from an empty house in the city. Empty but filled with cats of every size and colour. I can see you on your hands and knees, moving between them, loving the cats, stroking them, rubbing the tops of their heads. I can hear the rumble of purring, see the twisting supple bodies, raised tails, yellow and green eyes, slivers of pupils.

I drive west to the beach with my husband and sons. The national road crosses a river and rises steeply, cutting through plantations. I remember it was somewhere here that you were found. Somewhere here that you and India set up camp after you were both discharged from Tranquillity. After a week of moving from house to house, from friend to friend. After a week of being back on heroin.

I can see a dirt track where Mark might have parked his car after India phoned him. Before they walked up the hillside to a level section in the plantation. When India collected her clothes and duvet. When Mark looked for you. I can see the signs of habitation he described. Bedding. An apple. A bunch of grapes. A small axe. A pair of your jeans knotted at the legs to serve as a dustbin.

I can see you and India making a bed of pine needles, covering it with a blanket, lying under duvets on a warm January night looking at the stars through the branches. Eating fruit, listening to music, making love. I can't imagine the rest. I can't imagine what caused India to phone Mark, what led to her say: Come and fetch me, I can't keep up with this man.

You never asked Mark to fetch you. It was never your idea to go to rehab. It was Jolene's or it was your mother's. Each time you left Tranquillity you returned to the place you were happiest.

Mark says it was like you didn't have a skin to protect you. Heroin was your skin.

Tranquillity felt you needed certain things in place before they would discharge you. You met these requirements. You passed your learner driver's licence, got a job as a waiter, made a decision to file for divorce from Jolene.

You felt you needed certain things to survive in the world outside. You gave your mother a list. That's the only concrete thing I have – apart from one grainy group photograph – the list of appliances your mother bought for you:

Telefunken portable radio
Cleancut shaver wet and dry
George Foreman lean mean grilling machine
West Point vacuum cleaner
Russell Hobbes fan
Electrolux iron

And the list of appliances you pawned after your discharge: all of the above, plus one Sony CD Walkman and seventeen CDs.

Candlelit

after lengthy nocturnal ablutions involving contact lenses
and aqueous cream and floss and toothpaste and a final wee
the woman switches off the bathroom light and approaches
the candlelit bed where she removes her pyjama pants lifts
the weight of duvets and blankets and snuggles towards the
waiting body not as warm as he was when they first met and
he dived into bed every night as if into a swimming pool but
still warm and they kiss and he knows just where to touch and
pinch and she can smell the Mentadent P on his breath and in
two minutes it won't matter but now it does and she thinks of
him kissing their cat and burrowing his hands into its fur and
she can't stop herself lifting his fingers to her nose and sniffing
sniffily and saying are you sure you washed your hands and did
you scrub your nails

Rapunzel

Once in a time of peace, as the rainbows were just starting to fade, a taxi driver noticed a schoolgirl.

The schoolgirl was tall and strong. She twisted her hair into braids. Every fortnight she unplaited her cornrows and washed and conditioned her hair. Then she sat down at the mirror with her comb and a jar of coconut oil and created a new style. Sometimes the cornrows travelled back from her forehead like the rays of the sun. Sometimes they were lightning bolts. Sometimes they cross-hatched. She did the front and sides of her head, and her mother completed the back.

The first time the taxi driver saw her she had created a spiral above each temple. He hooted and waved. During school holidays she added hair extensions to create an elaborate lacy crown. Every time the taxi driver drove over the mountains to her coastal town he looked for her. She lived on a hill above the national road. He drove his minibus up and down the pitted streets around the high school until he found her. He hung out his window and called to her.

The schoolgirl ignored him. But you can only ignore a charming man for so long, her head was singing with his words. The day came when he made her laugh. The day came when she told him her name was Zel, when she showed him where she lived.

Zel's mother and grandmother disapproved of her older suitor. But at least he had a job. He brought food when he visited. He wasn't violent. He didn't drink. He only drove his minibus to their town once a week, they could get on with their lives in between.

Zel was a bright student. She studied hard, enjoyed maths and science and got a good matric. But there was only enough money for her brother to study further. There was only enough for him if Zel got a job in a restaurant kitchen.

The taxi driver collected Zel from the restaurant once a week. She untied her head-scarf and shook out her long braids as soon as he drove up hooting. She gathered them into a ponytail or a bun or a French plait. Her colleagues teased her about the driver. They made jokes when she put on weight.

On her days off Zel ran errands for her mother. It wasn't easy to get to the clinic. She might have missed an injection, she might have missed a few periods. She took a day's leave and joined the clinic queue.

The nurse admired Zel's braids. She did a urine test, an internal examination, she thought Zel was about four months pregnant. The nurse needed to do one more test, she needed Zel's permission, she needed Zel to understand what the test was for, what it meant to be positive.

The sun left Zel's heart. She went home and unbraided her hair. She borrowed an electric razor from a neighbour and shaved her head.

People thought Zel didn't want the baby. Don't worry I'll support the child, the taxi driver said, but she wouldn't look at him. We're here for you, her mother and grandmother said, but Zel turned away.

A crone who lived nearby saw Zel's shorn head, her haunted eyes. The crone helped out at the clinic. She took Zel aside. There was a potion, a new potion. Was she willing to try? She would be the first in town. The crone took Zel back to the clinic. The doctor mentioned strange words. She rattled off acronyms. She spoke about doses. One now, one when the baby was born, others at intervals afterwards.

Zel stayed away from her friends, she didn't speak to her colleagues, she was sure everyone was whispering about her.

The crone visited Zel. She said don't seal yourself off.

Zel's belly was too big to lean forward over the basin. She asked her mother to wash her short hair. She closed her eyes as her mother massaged her scalp. She handed her mother her jar of oil and comb. She asked for simple cornrows running from left to right. She told her mother about the positive test. When the last braid was plaited Zel no longer felt alone.

Zel's baby was born small and sickly. Zel loved him. The taxi driver came to visit. The taxi driver had lost weight. He looked at his skinny son, he looked away. He sent money now and then.

Zel took her baby to the clinic. The nurse gave him the potion as directed. He had the test when he was bigger. He got the wrong result.

Zel considered shaving her head again but the clinic doctor said there was new research, there were more potions. There was a potion to give the baby every day. There was still hope.

There were mothers who died. There were babies who died. There were others who survived. There were mothers who grew stronger. Mothers like Zel. She got a government job with medical aid. Her grandmother cared for the child while she worked. Her grandmother gave the little boy his potion. She never asked what it was for.

Zel took the potion too. She stayed strong and healthy. She wound her long braids around her head like a halo. She tied them into loops on the top of her head. She met a kind man. They had tests, they followed the doctor's instructions, they had a healthy daughter.

The taxi driver died. Zel was invited to his funeral. She wore a mountain range of braids with cornrows streaming to her hairline. Zel and her son travelled a long way to a neighbouring country. They were welcomed by the taxi driver's family. They sat beside his coffin. They sat beside his children. They sat beside his wife, beside his other women. They didn't speak about the driver. They didn't speak about the plague. They whispered about Zel's braids.

Visiting rites

You must stop at the boom. You must give your name, your phone number, your car's registration number and your friend's name and house number. You must wait while the security guard phones your friend and she confirms that you are known and wanted.

You must drive through an avenue of similar houses, over narrow bridges, and around traffic circles filled with gazanias and windflowers. You must find somewhere to park where the homeowners have not placed whitewashed rocks to prevent tyres from crushing their lawns.

Try to feel like a mud prawn. They feel welcome. Mud prawns have colonised the canals gouged into this island to create a suburb of waterfront properties. Fish have followed the prawns. Seahorses cling to the sea grass. A dolphin swam into the canals from the lagoon and out again.

Your friend came here from the mountains. In the mountains she walked barefoot and swam naked in icy streams. Her car was covered in dust and mud. Her hair was often unwashed to save water. She worked from a cabin in a clearing. People came to be healed by her hands.

Your friend's car is never dirty in this new place with its tarred roads and man-made beaches. Her hair gleams. She has a scar on her forehead from her first night here. She was lifting the lid of the built-in braai when it struck her.

Alphabetically

Attached

Her eyes and ears were the strings that controlled her. Without their messages coursing through her neural pathways making her face shine with understanding, blaze with disagreement, she was limp, extinguished. A crumpled marionette.

Aubade

Crossing your legs so your feet are beneath your knees. Placing your hands on the knees. Joining the palms at the base of the sternum. Softly close the top eyelids to meet the bottom eyelids. Descend the eyes towards the centre of the chest, the centre of the heart. Observe the body. As you breathe – a normal inhalation, a normal exhalation – maintain the lift of the spine. Feel the fullness of the chest. Feel the heart expanding as it lifts. Exhale to begin the chant. Inhale. *Om.* Spread and lift the chest. Bow the head to the heart. Release the hands to the legs. Slowly lift the head. Softly open the eyes.

Awnings

They sat on the stoep in the fresh air. He said wouldn't it be nice to sit here in summer? They bought a retractable awning they could roll out when they needed shade. He said wouldn't it be nice to sit here when it rains? A builder nailed perspex roof sheets over a wooden frame. The sheets collected dirt and algae but the chairs on the stoep stayed dry. They sat outside on a hot night. She said wouldn't it be nice to feel a breeze?

Gifts

She gives the young man raised by women her yellowed notes, a rare photograph of him as a child on his mother's lap, a fat envelope of newspaper reports concerning his father's assassination. She tries: 'I met your father a few times. He was young, loose-limbed – yes, with something of your physicality. But your mother did most of the talking. Your father hovered. He was guarded, taciturn, withheld approval.' She tries but she can't give the hero's son the one thing he wants. The answer to one question: What was my father like?

Mirror

She is programmed to repeat what she hates. A friend says: Put it this way. The woman squirms, goes home, and says it too. Over and over. Or put it this way, she says, helplessly. A long-haired acquaintance has no eyebrows. The woman stares, appalled. Then the woman moves her own hair out of her eyes and her fingers brush against a rogue eyebrow. A stiff whisker. She goes to a bathroom mirror and sees a silver antenna sticking out of her brow. An alien aerial. She starts patting her brows frequently, checking for bristles, yanking the long ones out with her fingers. She checks obsessively in her bathroom mirror which lights up only one side of her face. Tweezing away all offensive hairs is no easy task, many of their innocent neighbours are removed too. In a restaurant's sunlit mirror the woman sees what she has done. And she sees the work ahead on the other brow.

Plumbing

The nurses want to help. They insist on helping. They take the unhappy baby out of her arms. The ward is quiet, night-lit. Her narrow bed is cold. She lies on her back. She hears the water pipes crying. She gets up, dons gown and slippers and walks to the nurses' station at the end of the corridor. She looks through the large window at the nurses smoking. One is wearing a jersey over her uniform. A complicated jersey with loops of wool and bobbles. This nurse has a baby tucked into the jersey, against her chest. She is jiggling from one leg to the other while she smokes and pats the crying infant. Hers. The woman's stomach contracts, her Caesar scar throbs. She pretends nonchalance: 'I couldn't sleep, so I might as well take him,' she tells the nurse. She carries her smoky son back to bed fiercely, smugly: So the nurses couldn't settle him either.

Plunging

She drives home on a broiling autumn day, stops at a garage and pushes through the heat to buy water. The berg wind melts the petrol attendants. Their faces drip.

She has been away so long her pillow feels wrong. The distance from her side of the bed to the bathroom seems shorter. Her husband feels strange. His kisses are pointy. She holds him inside her for a long time, crouched over him, plastered to him, when she releases him he is hot against her stomach.

She wakes thirsty, needing to pee. Darkness so thick she can't tell if her eyes are open or shut. She moves towards the light coming from the bathroom window, takes a step towards the bathroom, then stops. Forces her eyes wide open. Forces her eyes to stare ahead: At the glow from the window above the landing; at the tiled stairs descending below her feet.

Pulsing

Her eyes keep drooping. She carries on reading with closed lids, making up sentences, paragraphs. She opens her eyes again but can't find her place. Then she finds her place but almost immediately her lids grow heavy. She puts down the book, switches off the light, and sleep deserts her. Squiggles pulse across her retinas. Paragraphs of text flash and melt into glowing words. She tries to relax, tries to sleep, tries to lie still. The words keep flashing. She gives up, switches on the light and reaches for her notebook, her pen. The words disappear.

She writes in her dreams. Words, sentences. She forces herself awake just long enough to write the words down. One perfect sentence. She leaves the light off, opens her notebook with its elastic bookmark, writes with her eyes shut, using large letters, leaving lots of space between and around the words. In the morning she reads: *She crawls into the space and closes the hole.*

Siren

He wasn't much to look at. Not tall. Not dark. Not chiselled. He sat at the table. Watched. Ate. Drank. Waited. He opened his mouth, released words. It was not what he said. It was resonance, timbre, molten treacle. It flowed through the women. They shifted, looked down, leaned forward. Humming birds drilled.

Spellbound

They gathered together to listen to a long limbed long faced cowgirl, beautiful and haunted in equal parts. She transferred pain into words. She wove her spell through prepositions. The overlooked words. The ins and ons and overs. She read for an hour. She offered to stop three times. They urged her on.

Structure

They gave him choices. Did he want his nappy changed? Would he like a banana or a pear? Would he like swimming lessons? They visited three nursery schools and he chose the one with the best swing. He wore jeans to high school, avoided sport, dropped maths for maths literacy. He chose to spend his weekends drinking with friends. He chose a best friend who went into an alcohol-induced coma. They gave him an ultimatum. He chose to leave home. He chose a school with blazers and kilts. A hostel where his only time alone was in his dreams. He chose to train so hard he puked, blacked out, made the team.

Symmetry

Women the same age. Women of a certain age. Mothers of teenagers close in age. One woman a teacher, one a student. One woman a writer, the other a reader of all her books. They meet at the row of basins and mirrors, exchange words of admiration and gratitude, display equal helpings of maternal pride. They excuse themselves, enter stalls a few doors apart, empty their bladders in synchronous urgency.

Wellspring

They experiment with energy in the dance class. They transfer it to a partner. Then one person stands with closed eyes in the middle of a crescent of dancers and everyone beams energy onto her. When it is the new woman's turn to face the crescent, her arms tingle, grow hot. Later they form a circle and skip forwards sweeping energy into the centre with their arms and hands. They toss it into the air and skip backwards, chi raining down over them.

Her dance class gives the woman energy. Her house doesn't. Her house has a fixed amount of creative energy for its two occupants. She waits for him to leave the house before she can begin. Or she gets busy first and feels the source streaming through her while he retreats to the garden. But usually he gets a head start and taps into the wellspring all day. By evening she is too tired to work or perhaps the daily quota is all used up.

The Good Housekeeping Magazine Quiz

1. Your husband's First Big Love is crossing an ocean to come and visit him after thirty years. Would you say:
    a. 'I've got so much work to do I can't talk about this now.'
    b. 'How did you get in touch with her anyway?'
    c. 'What does she want? To introduce you to your love child?'
    d. 'She's not staying here.'
    e. All of the above.

2. Your husband's FBL has booked a week's accommodation in your town. You will be away at a conference for five of these nights. Would you:
    a. Say: 'I've got so much work I can't think about this now.'
    b. Tell your best friend.
    c. Tell your sister.
    d. Tell a tableful of mutual friends who all take it in turns to cross-examine your husband with glee.
    e. All of the above.

3.	Your husband tells a tableful of friends that he sees FBL's visit as the biggest threat to his marriage in twenty-five years. His worst fear is that he will be attracted to her. Would you:

	a.	Say: 'Well I will be away at a conference that week so it's up to you.'

	b.	Say: 'Just make sure you don't rock our son's emotional stability. Remember he is in matric.'

	c.	Take comfort in the horrified looks on your friends' faces as they sing your praises and call the imposter names.

	d.	Turn cold when you see how serious your husband is when he says this.

	e.	Collect a pile of dirty plates to take to the kitchen.

4.	Your husband has photographs in his studio waiting for FBL's visit. They are pictures she gave him when she was seventeen. She is standing against a wall in baggy pants and a long-sleeved white T-shirt. Her hair is down in one and she is holding it up in another. She looks young and sweet and beautiful. Do you feel:

	a.	Threatened.

	b.	Threatened.

	c.	Threatened.

	d.	Threatened.

	e.	All of the above.

5.	Next to the photographs is a copy of a story he told her every night before they went to sleep. A story about a frog which he illustrated at art school. Do you:

	a.	Think: 'Well he tried to tell me the same story but I kept pointing out the non sequiturs and asking him questions.'

b. Think: 'They spoke different languages so maybe this was their way of communicating.'

c. Remember a publisher telling him the story did not have a focus.

d. Skim through it again and notice how many babies the frogs had.

e. Go back to your desk and try to work.

6. FBL is arriving in a week. Do you tell yourself:

   a. I could leave this town and get a full-time job. I could have a whole new life on my own.

   b. I could rent a little house near a surf break. My older son would come and stay with me in his holidays.

   c. I could move to a city. My younger son would come and stay with me in his holidays.

   d. But after a while I would start looking for a new partner. Would I find the same connection, the same contentment?

   e. I'll never have the same shared history with anyone.

7. It is your silver wedding anniversary three days before FBL arrives. Do you:

   a. Go out for dinner and speak frankly and at length about your relationship and how threatened you feel about FBL's visit.

   b. Listen to him say he is as nervous as you.

   c. Notice how thin he has become.

   d. Wonder if he's deliberately lost weight to look more youthful.

   e. Order another glass of wine.

8. FBL arrives in two days. Do you have:
   a. Excruciating neck pain.
   b. No appetite.
   c. Pain in your right nipple.
   d. Diarrhoea.
   e. All of the above.

9. FBL arrives tomorrow. Your husband says he thinks he'll go and have afternoon tea with her at her guest house. Do you:
   a. Say: 'For god's sake don't go rushing over there, wait for her to settle in and contact you.'
   b. Realise that you are just delaying the inevitable.
   c. Check his phone while he is in the shower and see he never read out the last line of her message: Hopefully see you very soon.
   d. Not mention that you checked his phone.
   e. Take anti-inflammatories for your neck.

10. It is the night before FBL arrives. Do you initiate sex and go down on your husband because:
    a. You want to.
    b. The tension is killing you.
    c. It might be the last time you want to.
    d. He won't be able to say he's not getting this at home.
    e. You might never make love with him again.

11. It is the morning of FBL's arrival. Your husband
    has spent the previous week planting fifty trees
    in the garden. He has tidied the lounge. He has
    left to bring FBL to your house for tea. Do you:

    a.   Busy yourself printing out reports for your
         work trip the next day.

    b.   Go to the loo.

    c.   Take another anti-inflammatory for your
         neck.

    d.   Wear ordinary clothes and no make-up
         because really you couldn't be bothered
         and perhaps this shows that you are not
         threatened.

    e.   Put a load of laundry in the washing
         machine.

12. As you are reading the Sunday paper at the
    kitchen table, your husband's car pulls up
    outside. You get up and open the front door.
    Do you:

    a.   See a heavy middle-aged woman. See your
         husband look at you with don't-worry-this-
         is-not-the-girl-I-used-to-know eyes.

    b.   Welcome her, make tea, ask to see pictures
         of her daughters, show her pictures of your
         sons.

    c.   Notice her tight clothes, gelled hair, new
         leather boots. Notice her even-toned skin.
         Notice the tension around her mouth.
         Notice how freaked out she becomes by a
         mosquito bite.

    d.   See her relax and become more ani-
         mated. Hear her similar views on child
         rearing to yours. See the way she looks
         at your husband. See the way he looks at

you. See how she is beautiful at certain angles. Feel the tension in your own mouth.

e. All of the above – so you excuse yourself to hang up laundry.

13. You, your husband, your younger son and Yael go to a seaside restaurant for lunch. Do you:

a. Insist your husband drives Yael so you can give your son a driving lesson.

b. Tell your son Yael is a friend of his father's from Israel. Watch with pride as he behaves charmingly throughout lunch.

c. Talk Yael through the menu.

d. Notice how she turns her back on your husband and faces you for most of the meal.

e. Notice how difficult she finds it to chew.

14. Your husband and Yael arrive home from the restaurant one hour after your son and you. Do you:

a. Let them talk some more on the stoep while you pack for your trip.

b. Give Yael some ointment for her mosquito bite.

c. Tell her it was nice to meet her. Mean it.

d. Watch her say: 'Thank you for all this.' Her hands raised and open, indicating what?

e. Tell her you'll be away for the week and your husband will be very busy looking after your son. Wonder if you should have said that.

15. After your husband takes Yael back to her guest house do you:
    a. Think about what she's done: chosen to leave her two daughters, husband, family and friends and come to South Africa to find closure with a boyfriend she knew thirty years ago.
    b. Realise she was vague about whether she was still living with her husband.
    c. Think about what she said: 'This is a present I am giving myself for my fiftieth birthday.'
    d. Feel her pain.
    e. Think about what she said about her siblings. How they are so jealous of her. How she was in therapy to deal with their hostility. Wonder what she told her therapist about your husband.

16. When your husband returns home, he makes you tea and you sit down to talk. Does he tell you:
    a. Yael told him she would have come to visit even if he had tried to dissuade her. She had re-read all his letters and found one where he told her he loved her.
    b. She wasn't interested in doing much tourist stuff.
    c. All she wanted to do was go over the past.
    d. He is grateful for how warm you were to her. She said she was grateful too.
    e. He will wait for her to initiate the next contact. He will look after your son while you are away. He will probably meet her for lunch a few times.

17. It is five nights later and you have just arrived home from your demanding conference. You spoke to your husband once during the week and he said FBL's visit was going well and she seemed to be happier. Now your husband walks through the door with a pink rose he was given at a relative's funeral. He gives you the rose, you put it in water and ask about his week. His face has a crumpled expression you've never seen before. Do you ask him:

   a. If it was a difficult week.

   b. Whether FBL wanted more from him at every meeting.

   c. Whether they had a lot of physical contact.

   d. Whether they had sex.

   e. All of the above.

Game farm

He came back home to build a road for his father. Two tracks of gravel that travelled a circular loop from the farm's entrance gate. It was the first game reserve in the area.

The father's plan was for visitors to stop halfway, walk through a milkwood thicket, climb a sandy hill to a lookout hut, and enjoy the sea view. There were parking areas overlooking a water hole where people could get out with their flasks of tea and binoculars and observe the zebra, wildebeest and bontebok. They could admire the fynbos and identify birds with the help of the list on the brochure.

Most visitors sped around the track in ten minutes. Some wanted their money back.

It was the Cape dune mole rats who liked the road best, especially the grassy strip between the gravel tracks. Every mole hill in the middelmannetjie meant a rodent had burrowed under a track. After a few vehicles had travelled over the burrow, the road would cave in, making it inaccessible to low-slung city cars. And the son and farm workers would have to shovel more gravel into the hollows.

There were natural predators on the farm: mole snakes, birds of prey, caracals. But the snakes took days to digest one thick-pelted mole rat. And the rodents were good breeders. The females popped out two or three pups twice a year. They didn't like sharing living quarters: one dune mole rat one burrow.

The farm's most visible endemic mammals were the bush-buck and grysbok. The father loved the bushbuck with their spotted flanks but felt most protective of the grysbok. A tiny African bambi. But caracal kept picking them off. A caracal, with all the mole rats it could eat, kept leaving behind its calling card of grysbok carcasses with just one haunch eaten.

The son bought dozens of traps and slaughtered three hundred mole rats. But the mole hills kept multiplying, the road kept collapsing.

After his father found the remains of yet another grysbok, the son baited a walk-in trap. Days later a snarling caracal hissed at him through the mesh of the cage. A glossy cat in the prime of its life. The most beautiful creature the son had ever seen close up. He photographed it. He put a bullet through its head.

Displays

Her trolley keeps clipping the edges of shelves as she turns a corner, slightly dislodging boxes at the bottom of promotional displays. She goes to two shops. The nudging and bashing has nothing to do with the breadth of the aisles or the faulty steering of the trolleys. She wishes a tower of tins would appear, instead of these built-in shelves of metal, these castles of cardboard. She would aim her trolley carefully to hit the most stable and dependable tin of the lot. And as the whole pyramid teetered and collapsed in a clattering mass which drowned out the in-store radio – and all the better if someone was hurt; all the better if it was her own blood – and people came rushing and asked *What happened? Are you all right?* she would answer truthfully *I'm not sure. No.*

What Nombuyiselo said

Ripple dressed quietly in the dark. She left for Cradock at dawn. She drove away from the lagoon, away from the ocean, through forests snarled with vines.

She stopped at Storms River. Checked her phone. Washed her hands in a basin decorated with leaves and flowers. Placed a coin in the saucer for the cleaner. She stared at her reflection, averted her eyes.

Rip drove east over bridges, under flyovers, past wind turbines. She drove through Port Elizabeth and alongside revetments and dolosse. She stopped again after the Zwartkops River. Bluewater Bay: the coastal scrub where the bodies of Matthew Goniwe and his comrades were found. The off-ramp led to a petrol station. The attendants argued about soccer as they filled her tank, wiped squashed insects off the windscreen. Rip parked, walked through the sliding doors, bought Coke Lite. She checked her phone in the toilet stall.

Colchester. The N10. Paterson. Dense thickets of thorny trees. Sloping Zuurberg Mountains. The red rock face of Olifantskop Pass. The red rock she crashed into. She was young then, playing hard, working harder. A young journalist driving to her first political trial. She must have fallen asleep at the wheel. She remembered the rock face rushing towards her, trying to turn away from it, then waking up upside down, her head resting on the car's padded ceiling, her seatbelt tight, dress bunched up at her waist. Alive. Lucky. Hitching a lift to the courtroom.

Rip felt her seatbelt cutting into her as she rounded the last corner of Olifantskop Pass, the same red rock where the security forces said they set up a temporary roadblock. Where a security policeman stepped out into a dark road with a torch to wave down a car with four occupants: Matthew Goniwe, Sicelo Mhlawuli, Fort Calata, Sparro Mkonto. Two headmasters, a teacher, a railway worker. Fighting to improve living conditions. Making Cradock ungovernable. Organising boycotts of schools, rents, white-owned shops. Replacing puppet town councils with street committees.

Rip's old dread of the security police resurfaced. Cold waves of fear that drained her of all warmth. The same ice that clenched her gut and chest when her car's tyres were stabbed, or she received anonymous hate mail, or heard the click of her tapped phone. When Ripple's sons asked her about those days her throat closed and she struggled to find a way to begin. What could she tell them? Her experience was nothing compared to the daily harassment, death threats, prosecution, imprisonment, detention without trial that the Cradock men endured.

Rip clenched her jaw and drove. She drove away from her nuclear family. She drove towards Matthew Goniwe. She pushed her foot down on the accelerator, chasing a younger version of herself. She had dressed for work then, skirts, black pants. Now she wore magic jeans which promised to flatten her stomach. She passed lucerne fields, aloes, flat-topped Karoo koppies. Old terror resurfaced seizing her neck and shoulders. She ate a handful of almonds, finished the Coke.

Ripple stared at the green fields. She tried to picture Matthew Goniwe's face in the torchlight as the men were handcuffed. She clasped the steering wheel. She stared ahead of her. She thought about Matthew under interrogation.

Still she drove. In the rear-view mirror the fields gave way to the turn-off to Cookhouse. Rip kneaded her neck. The first time she drove this way was to interview Nyameka Goniwe. Matthew was in detention. Nyameka was cloaked with exhaustion, her children clung to her. Nyameka spoke with calm, measured urgency: her husband was a man of conviction, a man of peace, a man who gave up boxing for yoga, a man who beat drunk school students who had looted a beer hall.

Of all the places Rip worked as a journalist she felt most awake in Cradock. Most alive. A witness to an extraordinary political mobilisation of an entire community. Even the toddlers had raised defiant clenched fists. She needed to go back there. She wanted to go back to a time before the slumbers of suburbia. She wanted to interview Nyameka Goniwe again, now she was the mayor of a united Cradock. She had sent a letter weeks ago, followed up with emails, left phone messages.

Rip remembered the dip in the road with the blue gums. The N10 climbed, levelled off. Cradock came into view: Lingelihle on the left for black people, rows and rows of identical tiny houses including lots of newer ones, the tips of the concrete pillars of the Cradock Four memorial breaking the skyline. Michausdal on the right for coloured people, slightly bigger houses, some trees. She drove into the town itself: ornate Victorian buildings, a grid of tree-lined streets parallel with the mud-coloured Great Fish River, spacious houses still mostly filled with white people.

Rip stopped at a B&B with a rose garden, climbed stiffly out. The housekeeper showed her to her room: a double bed with white linen and beige towels rolled into sausages. She opened the curtains, massaged her neck. Rip checked her phone: no messages, no calls. She dialled the Cradock municipality. The number rang and rang. She checked her emails, still no reply from Nyameka or her office. She dialled the municipality again: the executive mayor was in a meeting.

Rip walked to a restaurant, ate chicken salad, studied a map of the town. She walked to the freshly painted municipal building with its ostentatious gable and thought about asking to see Nyameka. She went to the Great Fish River Museum instead. She had been there before. She remembered the room filled with cots, life-sized baby dolls with chipped porcelain faces, intricate christening gowns. There were displays about the British Settlers, Voortrekkers, posters about Nelson Mandela's life.

Rip asked to see the Cradock Four Gallery. A humble shed in the museum's yard. The curator unlocked the door. Large full-body photographs of the men walked towards her from four pillars. The images of Matthew and Fort came from an iconic photograph taken the day they were released from detention. Rip had been standing beside the photographer. Their newspaper had sent the two of them to Cradock to cover their release, but not to interview the men, the 'listed' men, whose spoken and written words could not be published.

In the photograph Matthew, Fort and two comrades are walking towards the camera, towards Rip. They are casually dressed, relaxed, smiling, arms hanging down by their sides. Children are watching from either side of the dirt road. Women are walking out of a house carrying boxes on their heads. Small square houses with wire fences line the street. A sparsely vegetated Karoo koppie rises in the background. The picture says: free again. It says: these are the gentle men the government calls terrorists.

That was the narrative her newspaper reports told. Things were clear to her then: the apartheid security forces were bad; the voteless protesters were good. Several cuttings with her by-line were among the newspaper clippings, biographies, time-lines and photographs covering the gallery's three walls.

There was another narrative her reports hadn't told: the men's connections with the then-banned African National Congress. Fort was the grandson of ANC secretary general Canon James Calata. Matthew's brother Jacques was killed while fighting for the ANC's armed wing. At the same time as leading the Cradock Residents Association and seeking reinstatement as the local headmaster, Matthew was helping to organise the ANC's underground structures in the Eastern Cape.

Thirty years ago Rip had been careful not to ask too many questions about what people knew, or did, or planned to do. It was a time when just compiling a list of all the missing, poisoned and detained popular leaders was considered defiant.

Ripple drove to the Victoria Hotel for supper. The dining room with its red velvet curtains, fake silver candlesticks and fabric roses was filled with vintage car enthusiasts in town for a rally. Rip felt invisible. She exchanged text messages with her sons. Messages that made her smile. She ate quickly and left.

In the shower, hot water scalding her neck and shoulders, Rip asked herself why Nyameka should remember her out of the dozens of journalists she'd met. It was not as if Rip had kept in touch. Or covered major events. All she had to show for the last decades were a few scrapbooks of small town news. And two golden children. Sons she had always put first, hoping that if they felt loved and heard there would be two less damaged people in the world.

Sitting up in bed under the white duvet, Rip sifted through her Cradock assassinations file. She re-read the post-mortems:

Sicelo Mhlawuli, 36: A slit throat. *Right hand ... cleanly amputated immediately above the right wrist.* Multiple stab wounds in the chest, back and arms. *Death was due to blood loss, predominantly from the severed jugular vein ... The variation in the appearance of the stab wounds suggests that a variety of weapons was used.*

Sparro Mkonto, 33: A bullet in the head. A bullet in the chest. Multiple stab wounds. *Death was due to multiple injuries, the most significant being the gunshot wound to the head and the two stab wounds through the heart.*

Fort Calata, 28: Multiple stab wounds. *The cause of death was stab wounds to the chest involving the right ventricle of the heart and the pulmonary vein; the difference in dimensions of the wounds suggests that several weapons were used to inflict the injuries.*

Matthew Goniwe, 37: Multiple stab wounds. *The immediate cause of death was a stab wound which transfixed the right ventricle of the heart, resulting in massive intra-thoracic bleeding.*

Collectively the four men were stabbed sixty-three times. After they were murdered their faces and bodies were doused with petrol and burnt.

Two inquests, a press exposé of a state security instruction that Matthew and Fort be *permanently removed from society,* harrowing evidence before the Truth and Reconciliation Commission which refused to grant six security policemen amnesty – and yet those responsible were never charged.

On YouTube Ripple watched a filmmaker give a reason for the ANC government's unwillingness to act: a tacit agreement between the apartheid government and ANC that 'we won't air your dirty laundry if you don't air ours'.

On the verge of sleep, fragments of Ripple's Google meanderings returned: Sparro was a talented soccer player. Fort played in a band. Sicelo worked for an Oudtshoorn community newspaper. Matthew sent poetry and lively letters to an English professor. The final line of his poem These Walls seemed prophetic: *silence seals my soundless box.* Rip imagined the lives these men might have led in a different South Africa.

A face woke Ripple at three in the morning. Matthew's furrowed brow, bespectacled eyes, wide smile.

After breakfast Ripple packed and zigzagged her way through Lingelihle to the rough road with no signpost which led to the Cradock Four monument: four giant rectangular columns with long concrete shadows. It was only five years old but it felt sad. Neglected. Adjacent buildings designed as a tourist and small business centre remained empty, vandalised, stripped of fittings. A section of the security fence had been pushed over.

Rip drove to the Lingelihle cemetery where she had joined thousands of mourners as four coffins draped in the black, green and gold flags of the banned ANC were lowered into the stony ground. The police and army had watched from the road and surrounding hills. 'It felt like liberation day,' Nyameka told a filmmaker. That night the government declared a state of emergency.

There was no apparent layout for the cemetery, no paths. Most graves were simple heaps of bleached soil, covered with rocks, overgrown with brittle grass or thorny plants. Only the graves of families with funeral policies had granite slabs and headstones. A number of the granite graves had been smashed. Rip had read that the Cradock Four burial site had been repaired after suffering a similar fate.

Ripple tried to avoid stepping on graves as she made her way to the largest site. A spiky palisade fence enclosed four adjacent granite slabs and headstones decorated with fluted columns, pediments, Grecian vases. The headstones carried revolutionary words: *Your blood will nourish the tree of the soil that will bear the fruits of freedom.* And below the men's names, and their dates of birth and death, the sentence: *Ever remembered by families.*

Ripple remembered the widows at the funeral: Nyameka Goniwe regal in an ANC head-scarf, Nomonde Calata seven months pregnant with Fort's third child, Sindiswa Mkonto as small boned as a child herself, Nombuyiselo Mhlawuli's expression of rage and incomprehension.

Driving away from Cradock, after buying a toy windmill on the side of the road, Ripple lowered her hunched shoulders. She breathed deeply. She was relieved Nyameka had ignored her request to meet. Relieved she could avoid asking questions about who had looted the Cradock Four monument and smashed the graves. Relieved Nyameka would not have to list all her administration's achievements and explain all her thwarted plans.

Rip was glad she need not tell Nyameka about her own town, where wood and tin shacks clung to hillsides and road embankments. Where the rich kept their eyes on the lagoon. Where Ripple's own house faced the estuary.

Rip retraced her route, travelling south down the N10 and west along the N2. Driving home to her sons, her husband.

She thought how the Cradock Four had been separated from their wives and young children by their activism: nights and days away at meetings, months and years locked behind prison bars.

In a way the men's love for their wives had aided their abduction. After their political briefing in Port Elizabeth had ended at nine o'clock, Matthew had insisted on driving home in the dark, saying he spent too much time away from Nyameka. Sicelo, in Cradock on holiday, had come along for the ride at the last moment, to be with his childhood friend Matthew – and hoping to see his wife Nombuyiselo who was working in Port Elizabeth.

None of the widows had remarried.

Nyameka Goniwe told the Truth Commission: 'Healing takes a long time.'

Sindiswa Mkonto cried every time she was interviewed.

Nomonde Calata told her husband's killer: 'Fort was not only my husband to me, he was my brother, my friend. He was everything to me. And you took him away in such a cruel way.'

In Nombuyiselo's biography of Sicelo in the Cradock Four gallery, she included just two sentences about their family life: *Three children were born out of the marriage. The last born baby, Bantu, died in the same year as his father, 1985.*

But she told Fort's killer more. Rip watched the news video.

Nombuyiselo said: 'I know how it is to lose a loved one: you feel empty, powerless and live with pain all the time.'

6

Embers

It begins with drought. With hot dry winds. The aliens are dying. Thirsty oaks are riddled with beetles and fungus. Ring-barked wattle are falling over. Mite-infested rooikrans are releasing fewer seeds.

You wait for rain. You wait for texts from your son in the city. Your younger son who is happier every day, until the day that he is not happy at all. *I am just feeling some mental strain.* You say come home, where it's safe.

He arrives with the wind. A boiling north-westerly breathing flames into the pine plantations, spitting fireballs faster than your son can drive. Jay and you go outside into the wind to meet him. You smell the burning. The overcast sky is yellow. The air is hot. The essenhout is gesturing frantically. Singed pine needles are landing at your feet. Jay says: 'Go straight to the jetty.' He will warn the neighbours, he will meet you both there.

Hold your son's hand and run away from your garden towards the lagoon. Watch burning embers land on the road. Laugh, you have your coat, your handbag, your passports, your son's warm hand in yours. Run past houses, past speeding cars packed with dogs and cat-boxes. See the wind bend palm trees. Watch flaming bits of leaves and twigs fly through the air. Hear the roar of the gale, the pop of an exploding gas bottle. Feel the heat of the wind, the grit in your eyes, in your nostrils. Smell the smoke, the burning. Hold your striped scarf over your nose and breathe. See the dense clouds of smoke coming closer towards you – black, then grey, then white nearest the flames.

Walk down to the jetty. See its creaking wooden platforms rocked by the churning lagoon, the small boats fighting against their ropes. Crouch down low near the jetty, so the wind doesn't blow you over, until flaming coals and sparks rain down around you. Hold hands with your son and run. Let the wind blow you across a wetland of inter-tidal succulents and across a grassy commonage, until Jay phones and calls you back: 'Trust me.' Turn and run back towards the jetty, into the wind, into the smoke, the thick white smoke. Try to keep up with your son. Run towards the shape emerging from the smoke, the tall shape: Jay, his arms. Hold hands, the three of you, and run across the wetland. Make them stop. Dip your striped scarf into the water at the edge of the lagoon and hold it against your nose. Breathe in the ozone. Look straight ahead. Don't turn and watch flames licking the bone-dry wetland. Don't listen to the crackle of vegetation, the pop-pop of gas bottles as another house catches fire. Hold hands and try to keep up with Jay, with your son.

Run until you have to walk, until the smoke clears, until you see the rescue boats arriving at the jetty, until you are on one of these boats bumping into waves, until you spend a sleepless night in a guest house on the other side of the lagoon. Stand at the guest house window and watch tall pines lighting up like twinkling Christmas trees, oaks flaring into lanterns, gums blazing with eucalyptus oil. See the fire jump from trees to houses. See balconies and roofs fall away as every window lights up. Watch an alien ring of fire consume your town.

❖

And afterwards there is your smoke-filled house, your coughing cat. Your son in his room. The dragon comes back, consumes kilometres of acacia, devours homes and farms and plantations, swallows fynbos and milkwood trees. The hills are bare, blackened. The trees in your road are still smoking. The ruins of houses smoulder. Seven in your suburb. Two hundred in one township. One thousand homes gone. And seven lives.

You open windows in your smoky house, before you remember the smoke outside. You wipe only the surfaces you need, before the ash resettles. You make tea on a gas bottle. You make soup and curry with the food in the fridge, before it rots. You talk to Jay for hours. You read by candlelight. You get up at night to check outside. Looking for the orange glow. Sniffing for fresh smoke. You go to town only to buy food. Only to see Jay's sister, the charred shell of her house, the empty space where you ate Christmas dinner. Only to visit a nature reserve: a nuclear wasteland, the soil white with hot ash, the trees' black skeletons, the charred bones of bushbuck, empty tortoise shells. You make a list of the homeless people you know, you sit in your car in the driveway, charging your phone, texting some of them: *I'm sorry*.

You do nothing. You do nothing except knock on your son's door, offer tea. He is reading in bed. He is fine. You do nothing, while the good people pack parcels for the fire victims. Parcels of food with fizzy drinks and biscuits and sweets. Although many good people believe sugar is bad and do not eat it themselves. And neither do you, except in dark chocolate. You eat honey.

You do not leave your house, unless Jay or your son are home. Because people who refused to evacuate saved their homes. Because your neighbour saved his house, then yours. He quenched your burning fences, your compost heaps. Someone must always be home to stand guard. The bush across the road flared up again. The avenue of charred oaks and blackened gums will not let anyone forget. The pine stump near the church cannot be quenched. You do not leave the house except to buy food. Except to have one hot shower in a suburb that still has electricity. Except to go to a lecture about aliens and honey bees.

The bees that escaped the fires are starving. The good people are feeding them sugar water. The lecture concerns which saplings to plant to feed the honey bees. Which trees will grow the quickest. The tree expert suggests flowering gums. The hall erupts. The pale-skinned people filling the seats know alien trees are bad. They must be eradicated. The audience is incensed. Righteous. 'No more bloody Australians.' They blame the aliens for the fire, the Californian pines, the Australian acacias. They rant without irony. Although they too crossed seas to put down roots, they or their ancestors. Although it was their pale-skinned countrymen who imported the aliens. Your pale-skinned countrymen.

❖

It returns with a dragon of smoke. A sleeping dragon that wakes when you wear your striped scarf. A sniff of smoke even though you have washed it twice.

It returns with a loud noise or a virus. It hardly matters which. What matters is that you are interrupting people, talking over their conversations, talking louder than you should. You are no longer listening, you are lip-reading. You are hearing what you think is being said. You are guessing. Your younger son is feeling better. He is feeling better every day. You think that is what he says. You believe that is what he is saying.

It returns with a spread of green slowly reclaiming the dead hills. The green of recovery. The relief. Until the saplings are examined. Until most are identified as aliens.

Notes

While some stories in this collection name actual people and places, and others contain fragments of text from newspapers, liturgical texts, court cases and academic papers, they remain works of fiction. They do not pretend to be accurate in detail or chronology, and events and characters have been imaginatively transformed.

❖

The epigraphs – used with the authors' permission – come from Lily Hoang's *A Bestiary*, Cleveland State University Poetry Centre, © 2016, page 44, and Ivan Vladislavić's *The Loss Library and Other Unfinished Stories*, Umuzi, © 2011, page 30.

❖

Dolphins left a chocolate in the fridge contains lines from poems in *Songs of Experience, Milton* and *The Marriage of Heaven and Hell* by William Blake (1757–1827) and mentions his paintings *Jacob's Ladder* and *Elisha in the Chamber on the Wall*.

Hypocrites quotes from the Anglican *Book of Common Prayer* and *Hymns Ancient and Modern*.

Amnesia uses slightly edited extracts – in which names are removed and punctuation is altered – from the following newspaper reports: 'A hill-side scar where a house once stood', *Weekly Mail* of 26 February to 3 March 1988, page 7, and 'Even if members go on rampage … there is little Inkatha can do', *Weekly Mail* of 19 to 25 February, 1988, page 7. Reprinted with permission from the *Mail & Guardian*.

Separate schedules includes portions of a statement sent to the Native Affairs Department in 1943 by Jan Stemmett, a temporary foreman at Vulcanus Trust Farm in the Pietersburg district: 'I personally was continually doing my best to persuade the Natives not to take the law in their own hands but they all stated that the land belongs to them and they could plough where they liked and as much as they liked … [They] state [that] the land belongs to them and their grandfathers and they can do what they like.'

Transvaal Province, Records of the Secretary for Native Affairs, 3799 2567/308 (I), statement by temporary foreman at Vulcanus, 28.1.1943. **Separate schedules** also refers to *The Kruger National Park: A Social and Political History*, by Jane Carruthers, University of Natal Press, © 1995.

A garden full lists fragments of Annexure A29 from the State versus Theunis Christiaan Olivier, Case no SS 70/2007 in the High Court of South Africa (Cape of Good Hope Provincial Division).

Contractions contains lines from *The Child who Was Shot Dead by Soldiers at Nyanga* by Ingrid Jonker (1933–1965) as read by President Nelson Mandela at the opening of the first democratic Parliament on 24 May 1994. From *Selected Poems/Ingrid Jonker;* translated from the Afrikaans by Jack Cope and William Plomer, Human & Rousseau, © 1968.

Stone cold lists fragments from Annexure A36 from the State versus Heinrich Urwyler van Rooyen, Case no. SS 55/2007 in the High Court of South Africa (Eastern Circuit Court held in Knysna).

Aubade in **Alphabetically** is an edited transcript of yoga teacher Roberta June Lombardi's instructions.

What Nombuyiselo said, like the rest of this collection, is a work of fiction. The writer had no appointment with the former executive mayor of Cradock, Nyameka Goniwe. The story refers to the (contested) police version of where the abduction of the four men took place. The iconic photograph of Matthew Goniwe, Fort Calata, Mbulelo Goniwe and Madoda Jacobs was taken by Colin Urquhart and appeared on the front page of the *Eastern Province Herald* on 11 October 1984. The post-mortem reports, which were presented at the inquests, are numbered K0817531, K0817616, K0817744 and K0817745, and dated 18, 19, 22 and 22 July 1985. Other sources consulted include *Eastern Province Herald* and *Weekly Mail* newspaper reports; Truth and Reconciliation Commission records and videos available online; *The Cradock Four* film (Shadow Films, 2010) and director David Forbes's comprehensive website www.thecradockfour.co.za.

Acknowledgements

Grateful thanks to the editors of literary journals where the following stories were first published.

What Nombuyiselo said, Separate schedules and **Tongue-tied** appeared in *New Contrast*. **Jay & the lynx (Hugo and the Lynx)** and **The Good Housekeeping Magazine Quiz** in *Volume 1 Brooklyn's Sunday Stories*. **Riptide** in *The Drum, A Literary Magazine for your ears*. **I was wearing jeans** in *Type/Cast Literary Journal*. **Carousel** and **Peripheral** in *Itch the Creative Journal*. **Amnesia** in *Aerodrome*.

Shards was runner-up in the *Problem House Press* contest in 2016. An earlier version of **Dolphins left a chocolate in the fridge** was long-listed for the 2017 Short Sharp Stories Anthology *Trade Secrets*.

Thank you:

Colleen Higgs and Modjaji Books for the gift of this book, Alison Lowry, Jesse Breytenbach and Andy Thesen.

Stacy Hardy, brilliant and generous thesis supervisor, for insights into my post-thesis stories and global reading recommendations.

Every student, lecturer and visiting lecturer on the Rhodes MACW programme from 2014–2016, and the coordinators Robert Berold and Paul Wessels who taught writing through reading, so the learning never ends.

Stacy Hardy, Joan Metelerkamp and Henali Kuit for reading and commenting on the manuscript.

My wordsmith family Irene, Nikki, Simon and Julie. And Leon our cheerleader.

Leo and David, most wonderful children and adults.

Guy, most of all.

'In the blue-black world of Bekker's South Africa the legacy of the past inscribes its history on all bodies. The bodies of chain-smoking reporters in "unpredictable garments", of itinerate oboe players in the City of Roses, of baby starlings chucked through the dairy window to discourage the rats, all these and more bear upon them the marks of violence, of suppression, of life lived fitfully as if beneath a pall of smoke. And yet, this book's greatest strength is not the tenacity of the smoke but of the life that struggles through it.

'In a dazzling coil of interlinked tales Bekker mines the loaded seam between what we witness of the historical world amassing around us and what we internalise of that history into our remarkably unremarkable lives. In fairy tales and elegies, flash-bulb bright vignettes and elegant absurdities, *Asleep Awake Asleep* imagines the world as a response to the dream of self. It dares us to speculate on what the future may look like when that same self is no longer the property of history but its own true thing, blinking in the light.'

– Sarah Blackman, author of *Hex* and
Mother Box and Other Tales

Printed in the United States
By Bookmasters